The Seven Of Us

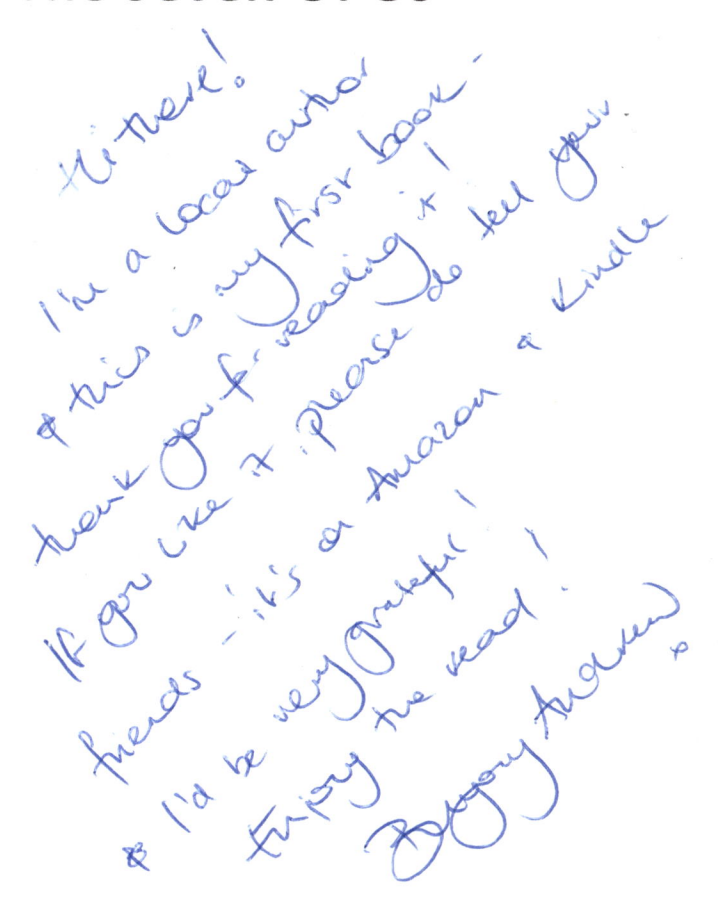

Hi there!
I'm a local author & this is my first book. Thank you for reading it!
If you like it, please do tell your friends – it's on Amazon & Kindle & I'd be very grateful!
Enjoy the read!

Gregory Andrews x

At sixes...

Simon

It must be before 6 am when Ella gets out of bed. I only know this because she strokes my face tenderly before kissing me gently from the wrong side of the bed – otherwise I wouldn't have noticed that she was up and awake. There are two main reasons for me not noticing – firstly, I always sleep like a log, and secondly, for someone who is tall and awkward around pretty much everyone, pretty much all of the time, Ella can move like a cat.

I have no idea what time it is when Alina slips into our bed, but when she throws her arm over me and mutters something into my neck about Christiana, I am barely conscious for long enough to recognise that the room is a little lighter. I am halfway through the first cup of coffee and well into my second slice of toast and marmalade when I figure that Christiana had probably climbed into bed with Alina at some point in the night, and Alina – being shackled with a shuffling snoring teenager (possibly not today, but that was verbatim her words at other times) – took refuge with me as soon as she could.

About half an hour later, and I am deep into the newspaper and my second cup of coffee, this suspicion is confirmed as first I hear two doors slamming upstairs – teenagers being unable to close a door any other way, apparently, signifying Christiana leaving Alina's room and returning to her own – and shortly afterwards Alina staggering into the kitchen grasping for the handle of the coffee pitcher. She stretches up briefly on tip toe to kiss me on the cheek as she passes and sits herself opposite me at the table. She looks exhausted and lays her head in the crook of her arm, face turned towards her mug so that she can smell the coffee. I have seen her like this before, obviously – living with a nurse you get used to seeing them exhausted, and I also know that no matter how pale and drawn she looks now, she will begin her metamorphosis soon and the figure leaving the house in about an hour's time will not remotely resemble the creature dribbling onto the sleeve of her pink fluffy dressing gown, blonde tangled hair pointing in all directions except for the right one.

First the slam of an upstairs door and then the front door slamming as Christiana leaves has the dual effect of making Alina start and waking Jack. Alina leaves her seat slowly and takes her coffee with her as she crawls back up the stairs, as Jack begins a sustained wail.

People always want to know about the sleeping arrangements, so I may as well get that out of the way. We all have our own bedrooms and our own privacy. Sometimes I will go to my bed and find Alina waiting there for me, often fast asleep, baby monitor winking away on the bedside, and all she will do is stir as I get in and throw her arms around me to sleep on my shoulder, just like she did on that first time in my old flat. Whenever we have made love, it is still always loving and tender. Even though we live in such strange circumstances I have come to realise that our love for each other never went away and now has deepened and strengthened. She is a strong and proud woman and a wonderful mother, and I am proud of her.

I find Ella in my bed a little more frequently. She has made good on her promise to never let go of me and I don't think that she ever will. I think sometimes I still see hints that she still has her reservations about herself, and I sometimes wonder if she feels like she made the wrong decision to stay with me, and to be honest I lack the courage to ask her. In all honesty I wonder if one day she will tell me that she is going to leave the home and none of us would try and stop her if that is what she wanted. I know she loves me in her quiet way, she will often reach out and squeeze my hand sometimes if, say, we are in the kitchen, and when we share a bed together, she wants to be held, and will hold on tightly to me, as though reminding herself of the promise she made to me and that I made to her.

The question people always really want to ask is whether we go to bed all together, and whilst I find this kind of questioning really rather rude the answer is no, we don't. I would not want that, and I really can't see the appeal. Truthfully, I don't. As far as I am concerned that is all I need to say on the matter.

There is no fighting about who sits next to whom, who goes to bed where or anything like that. Some days Alina and I will be curled up on the sofa, some days it is Ella, some days it is both. Both seem happy to hold my hand and there seems to be no enmity there, as far as I can tell; there seems to be an unspoken understanding – some sort of intuition about who needs to feel loved the most at the time. We have done social things together, and apart – some of our friends understand, some don't, some think that Ella is the lodger, and she doesn't seem to be bothered in the slightest that they do. They both seem to get along well with each other, which I found it very hard to accept to begin with, but I suppose neither feels threatened by the other, neither feels left out, and, importantly, I'd imagine, neither feels favoured. They both show me affection in their own ways, whether the other, or anyone else for that matter, is present or not. To be frank, I haven't overanalysed how it all works in case such analysis proves its undoing – what I do understand is that I am very lucky to have so much – I don't just mean having Ella and Alina in my life and in our home but living in what feels like an environment of genuine deep-rooted love that we seem to all have for each other, I know, is a rare thing indeed.

Christiana and Mama (I call her that too, not least of which because I still don't know her first name) treat me as the man that Alina loves and that is enough for them both. I have helped Christiana with her maths homework and moved furniture about, then back again, or unpacked boxes, or hung shelves, according to Mama's translated direction – she hasn't learned English, but she is getting better. Ella treats Christiana like a sister, and although being the younger one of the two it seems to be Christiana that provides all the fashion and shopping advice, in the same way, I suppose, that Anna and Sabine once did. Anna has been a regular visitor, as is Grace, and Sabine and Olek have even visited us once already. Sabine fussed over Jack like a grandmother and insisted that she would be known as Mimi as soon as the baby was old enough, Olek shook my hand firmly before pulling me into an embrace. Alina seemed taken aback by this until he did the same to her and Ella, and Sabina insisted that they immediately all go baby clothes shopping. I am yet to meet Roman – I expect I never will.

Baby Jack, as one might expect, is the apple of his Father's eye. I think secretly or not that every man wants to have a son, and I have my wish. He is going to be a handsome young man one day, as his features have taken on the best of Alina and I – that is to say, he looks entirely like her, right down to the blonde hair and beautiful face, except instead of his mother's blue, it looks like he has favoured my brown eyes – they seem to get darker every day.

Don't ask me how it works, or why it works – but it does. We all have our own lives and then come back together at home, and we are, to all intents and purposes, a family. We look out for each other, look after each other and, yes, we love each other too.

I am disturbed from my reverie on our living arrangements by the noise of a car pulling up outside. From here I can see our short driveaway but there is nothing there, so I step up to the window to see a pale blue hatchback I don't recognise pulled up at the side of the road. The strange thing is that it looks like Dee getting out of the driver's seat. The car itself obscures the driver partially, but I could swear that it is her.

Dee has not been in touch with me since long before we moved, but then I didn't tell her I was going anywhere. Still, if she needed to contact me my telephone number is the same. The days of hotels are long since over for us. The rambunctious, some might say edgy sex life that we had is a definitely a thing of the past. I would like to hope that we are still friends, and I think my new living situation would help her to determine that I am just as bad a bet for her as I once told her I would be; anyway, last I heard from her she seems to have made the sane choice to work on her marriage rather than on flights of fancy. Reflecting, I suppose I still love her in some way, perhaps not as much as I did, but she always knows how to find me if she needs me. It might have been a while, but I like to think I would not let her down.

The more I watch the pale blue car, the more convinced I am that it is Dee — which, in itself, is strange as she usually travels everywhere on the tube. By now Dee, if it is her, is at the back of the car and even more strangely appears to be wrestling a very large suitcase out of the boot. I had better go and see what is up. Whatever it is I'm certain that there's something of a story in this.

Simon, January 2014

Ella

It wasn't because we were poor, or because we were hungry, or I was particularly a rebel or anything like that, but I had decided that I had to run away. I had to, there was no other choice. And once you have reached the conclusion that you only have one choice, the thing to do then is to work out how best to put that choice into action.

The farm where I had grown up with my parents had been in my family for centuries, or so my father would say, but then he would always say it with a look in his eye, the way that he did. He could very well be telling the truth, though – the buildings are all an old red brick that I haven't seen anywhere else around and all of the buildings are in various states of repair – the only one without any obvious faults is our home, pretty much central to farm at the end of a long dirt road track through the trees. All I had known up until the age of 17 was that it was where we lived and where my father and mother tended to the apple farm, year after year. Many times, I heard about how my father's brother, Uncle Olek, had been the one that should have taken the farm on when Grandpa died but according to my father "apples were never good enough for Olek". Even though Olek must have left 15 years earlier, he would always say it with such bitterness.

Mama was always more forgiving of Uncle Olek, and the times I saw him in Lutynia I always remembered a smiling man, full of life, light, and energy. It was almost as if God had determined that there was only so much light and life to share between the two brothers, and that Uncle Olek had got Roman's share too. I would always remember Sabine too, graceful, and beautiful who would visit with Uncle Olek, bringing with her her own light and life. Naturally, my father disapproved of Sabine, and I can remember listening to my parents argue after Olek and Sabine had left the farm one summer and hearing my father shouting about "that whore Sabine" and her taking Olek away from the farm where he belonged.

That was an important theme for my father – where people belonged. Olek belonged on the farm taking charge of the bookkeeping and managing the farm hands, whilst Roman belonged out in the orchards or in the tool shed. Mama belonged in the kitchen or in the bedroom, feeding the working man and making him tall strapping heirs to take over the farm when he was too old to manage the farm himself. I don't think he ever forgave her for never producing the son that he wanted, and he never forgave me for being the last of his two children and for causing so much trouble during my arrival in this world that Mama would never bear children again.

He never really could make me fit somewhere that he thought I 'belonged' – my sister, the beautiful Grazyna – was his princess, his showpiece to the world, the girl that would marry a wealthy man who would take the troubles of the farm from his shoulders instead of the heir that would never come, and leave Roman to return to his orchards and machines. She had the same blonde hair that I did, the same green eyes that I did and the same pale skin that I did, except on her it all looked like something from a fairy tale and on my it looked like something put up to scare birds. Her hair cascaded in ringlets and curls, mine stayed flat and cut short so that I didn't have to fuss with it in the morning. Her eyes looked out from under long blonde and almost invisible lashes, mine shrouded by a semi-permanent frown. Her skin like alabaster, mine like malnutrition.

I was the tall, skinny, flat chested, awkward girl far too interested in books and study. I remember the number of times he would tell me to get my head out of those books, girl, and help your mother. Girl – almost like it was an insulting word to be said with a sneer. I remember one summer he tried to make me into the son he never had, showing me the tool sheds and machinery, and talking to me endlessly about seasons, pests, diseases, pressing and sieving, but the only aptitude he ever found useful was that I could help him with his books and numbers, a subject he was only vaguely familiar with at the best of times. I must have been twelve years old then, sat at my father's, and his father's, old writing desk, feet barely touching the floor, adding and subtracting the figures that meant next to nothing to him. It was the only job he found use for me on and the only job he ever asked of me from that summer onward.

I can remember the smiles of the men when they would come to collect their wages to see me, pencil in hand, counting out the zloty and groszy into little orderly piles and writing it all down in a book. "Little Lebski" they would call me, but never in front of my father lest they were on the receiving end of one of his long looks, followed by noticeably less available work in the coming weeks. It was a nickname that Sabine picked up on one of her visits and spent the whole summer calling me "little Lebski", much to the obvious annoyance of my father but to the great delight of the men.

No one crossed my father – not Mama, not me, not the men. Of course, Grazyna never needed to cross father, her every wish catered for and her whole life planned out before her. Only Uncle Olek, the only man I met in Lutynia who didn't care what my father thought of him or what he did, and Sabine for whom whatever my father thought about anything was of no concern of hers.

It was easy enough to get together the money I would need – my father had little interest in the bookkeeping when he had had to do it, but now he had me to do his sums for after school he had no interest whatsoever.

Here and there I'd add a little bit to the book for what we had paid out, here or there a little less for what we had been paid – never so much that could cause alarm, but certainly enough that even a casual cross referencing would have shown up. For months I collected, stored and hid. And counted – the number of times I must have counted that money whilst I was collecting it, working out what I would need to get to where I wanted to go, working out the routes I would take and the means by which I would get there, all the time with a knot in my belly thinking that I would be discovered, that for some inexplicable reason my father would decide that he needed to review his books, or check up on that last invoice or review the pay history of the men or.... I gave myself so many reasons why I would be found out, but the simple truth is that I belonged to the books and the books belonged to me, both of us out of the way, and he belonged to the orchards – two circles of existence that were never meant to cross.

Even with my lack of caution it took over a year to get enough money together – from the autumn of 1992 to the spring of 1994, just after the winter had passed. Over a year of stomach knotting, walking around thinking that everyone knew what I was up to and what I was planning, and the ever-decreasing circles of thought that if they all know what I am doing, then why don't they stop me? It's because they don't care about me, and they want me to go. They've always wanted me to go.

He has always wanted me to go.

I am cursed for being both the daughter he never wanted and for not being the son he can never have.

The further down this path that my thoughts take me, the easier and in some ways the harder it gets to contemplate what I am planning – easier because I am quite sure won't be missed, harder because something will mean that it won't work out for me because nothing ever has. I feel worthless and unwanted, not pretty enough to be another princess and not hardy enough to be the boy my father wishes I had been. The knotting in my stomach means I am eating even less than usual – I think that if I have one mouthful that I am going to throw up, and Mama notices me getting even skinnier. By the end of winter 1987 I was six feet tall but weighed less than sixty kilos. Mama always tries to convince my father that I should be seen by a doctor even though I protest against it – father tells her it would be a waste of money and that she should just make sure I eat more. One night I hear them arguing about it from my room before I hear a ringing slap and a crash – father is having no more said on the subject and has ended the argument the way he knows how. The following morning, he is out in the orchards before I wake up and Mama implores me to eat something, and I can see tears in her eyes above a swollen cheek. I force down some bacon and some bread and see the relief in her face – then feel guilty when I hide around the back of the tractor shed and push my fingers down my throat the minute I am out of the house.

I have to go, and I have to go soon.

The last few weeks I make as many preparations as I can – I make sure that I have my travel documents ready, and I know the timetable for the buses from Wroclaw to Berlin. I start packing away a few things that I'll need – some clothes, a picture of me, Grazyna and Mama on Mola Beach in Kolobrzeg from a holiday when we were little – Grazyna is showing off her pink swimming outfit to the camera whilst

Mama holds me on her lap in an oversized white sunhat. We all look happy, and it is one of the few things that I have that can usually make me smile. I pack books and stash money in various places – inside a shoe, in a side pocket of my bag, in a little purse covered in glittery sequins that I must have had since I was five, in my jacket pockets and I make ready.

Not surprisingly, all the men know me as I have been handing out their pay for the last few years. It's easy enough to persuade one of them to drop me off in Wroclaw one morning, probably next week, and to not mention it to Roman. I ask Tomasz as he is nearly my age, probably no more than a year or two older than me, and is one of the newest employees on the farm – although I have seen him many times coming here with what must have been his brother when Tomasz was little, and I know that he rides to work on his brother's old scooter rather than take a lift from one of the others. He is quieter than the rest too.

"Sure, sure," he says when I ask him, "doing anything nice?"

"Oh, just seeing some school friends," I tell him, "I might stay over and have dinner with them, you know, catch up."

"Sure, sure," he says again, and looks nervous.

"Is that alright?"

"Yes, sure, sure...if, you know, one night, perhaps in the summer?...you know, I, err...I wondered..."

"I don't think Roman would approve," I say to him as kindly as possible, "but thank you for asking," I add after a second of delay. And I mean it.

"Oh…OK…well, yes, see you next week then" he says and hurries off.

It is not that I don't like Tomasz or boys in general, but I'm not about to make a promise that I know I can't keep. And besides, in truth, Roman would not approve.

The morning comes when I have decided that today is the day. I arranged with Tomasz the day before that he would come early, take me to Wroclaw and then head back to the farm. I offer him some money for his time and trouble, but he refuses to hear of it. I feel worse for turning him down at that point than I did at the time. It is one of my most pleasant memories of Lutynia, that scooter ride on a bright, clear and crisp morning to Wroclaw, sitting behind Tomasz looking over his bright red helmet, wind in my face and my heavy little case tied onto the back with string. Tomasz' red helmet – I'll always remember that, he had terrible teasing from the other men about it. "He looks like a giant cock!" one of them said once, to much laughter. "Don't be an idiot," said another, "look at the size of him, he looks like a little tiny cock!". I hoped that kind-hearted Tomasz wouldn't get in trouble, and I told him as he dropped me off not to say a word to anyone, especially not to Roman. He probably thought I meant because of the trouble it would make for him, taking the boss's daughter on the back of his scooter, but I knew that when they worked out what I had done, I would not want Tomasz' kind heart be the cause of him losing his job or having a beating from my father.

I kissed him on the cheek, thanked him and watched him turn back for the farm. He looked back once as he set off with a half-smile, half-worried expression, but then he was gone out of sight around the corner, and I was alone.

That is one of the last things I remember about Wroclaw – Tomasz' little scooter with his bright red helmet disappearing from view. I wasn't sure of it at the time, but that was the last time I would see Wroclaw.

Dee

I can remember the very first time I saw him. It was the day of starting my first proper job after university, my first day of real responsibility of earning a salary and paying bills, the first time I would be fully responsible for me. I felt relieved that the study had not been in vain, excited at the prospect of working in a hospital saving lives and here I was entering the employment market as a fully-fledged member of the post-grad working elite.

Maybe not saving lives as such, but certainly in the same environment as people that *were* saving lives and helping them to do just that.

Unfortunately, the morning had not gone to plan – I just could not get my hair to go right ("got to make a good impression on your first day" Sarah had said), forgotten to take an umbrella with me or even a rain hat or even a plastic bag, for God's sake, so had been caught up in one of London's brief downpours with nothing to save me. Add to that the crush of the Tube and a fifteen-minute delay whilst the train sat in the tunnel between stations, I ended up stumbling into my first day of induction dripping wet, late, with ruined hair.

The lecture hall, such as it was, looked more like a community centre than a formal place of learning. I somehow had expected a more grandiose setting – this is, after all, a venerable and prestigious London hospital, but the hall is all plaster board walls and uncomfortable looking rows of chairs set out in neat little rows. As I cast my eyes over the rest of the room you couldn't help noticing the tall man in his thirties, carelessly sat sideways on in one of the chairs, one leg dangling over the arm like he was some teenager, gazing out of the window whilst everyone else sat primly in their seats, straight on, making polite conversation with each other or seemingly engrossed in their appointment letters. A few heads turned as I came in, then looked away quickly.

He didn't look up at all.

I straightened myself up a bit and walked down the central aisle to find a seat. As I got to almost level with his chair, he just turned his head, looked at me with a broad grin on his face and said, "It's alright, it hasn't started yet which is not unusual for an induction programme. Besides, I'm a veteran at these things and if there's anything you miss, I'm sure I can fill you in after. There's usually very little of interest", then he gave me a wink and stuck his hand out.

"Simon", he said – as though this was all the information I would ever need.

"Hi", I said, "I'm Denise" taking his hand and shaking it.

"Pleased to meet you."

And that seemed to be it – I carried on walking and went and found a seat near the back of the room. I sorted myself out and tried doing something with my hair which was a total mess. As I put my compact mirror down, I saw that he had turned in his seat and was unashamedly looking straight at me. I must have blushed which prompted another enormous grin from him before he turned back to look out of the window again.

He was right about one thing, there was truly little of interest as we had the this-is-what–your-induction-will-cover talk, the obligatory health and safety talk, the fire procedure talk, the emergency numbers talk and the three hours it took to deliver this seemed to take three days.

But there he was, still sitting side on in the chair, almost smiling to himself as this deluge of drudgery rolled over us. Unlike many of us he is not taking any notes or reading any hand-outs and as far as I could tell, not paying any attention to the multifarious slides and presentations that washed over us. He almost seemed as if he were in a different room, like he was not really part of what was going on around him. Whilst the rest of us either looked nervous, lost, or bored, he seemed almost serene. I could not help but wonder about him a bit – who he was, what he did – and before I knew it, I was thinking about the size of his hand as he had taken mine.

I actually said out loud "Oh, stop it" before realising what I had done and blushing profusely as heads turned.

"Are you alright?" said the lady at the front, and to this day I could not tell you what she was presenting to us at the time.

"Fine, thank you", I squeaked, and the heads turned away. All except his – I looked up from where I had bowed my head straight into those eyes again and a look held for one second, two, three...then another broad grin before he turned away.

"Are you comfortable sitting like that?" the lady at the front says to him. "Quite, thank you." he replies. "Wouldn't you like to sit straight?" she tries, "I couldn't sit like that."

"No, I wouldn't, thank you though," and from the tone of his voice I think he is probably smiling at her as he says it, and I can't help smiling to myself at this little exchange too.

Once the day is over and I'm back at the flat I tell Sarah all about my day and "this guy, I think his name is Simon" and all about how he didn't seem to be taking anything seriously. Unfortunately, Sarah has always had the ability to see straight through me, partly because I have a tendency to blush too often, and I think this is what makes her pick up on him straight away.

"You fancy him, don't you?" she says.

"I do not!" I say hotly. A can feel my face flush even before the denial is out of my mouth.

She laughs loudly, but kindly – "I know you Dee," she says, "I know when you're trying to cover up for yourself and, more importantly, I know when you fancy a guy. If it hadn't been for me, you and Benny would have never got together."

This is probably the first time since this morning that I have thought of Ben, and I can feel myself blushing again. Ben, Sarah and I have been through university together and Ben has been my boyfriend for nearly all of that time. We've promised ourselves that once we both have jobs, we're going to get married. Reminding myself of this, I pull myself together a bit.

"I do not fancy him," I say, "he's just a bit odd. Not the sort of attitude you'd expect from someone on their first day of work. Besides," I add, as if to give evidence that there is no way I could possibly fancy him, "he's got to be pushing forty." (adding in my head "he's not, at most he's thirty-one, maybe thirty-two").

Sarah gives me that sideways look she uses when she's sizing someone up, and I am grateful that she pursues it no further than a "Hmmmmmm" – after watching a funny film about ghosts Ben and I started calling it her Pirate Look, watch the film and you'll see what I mean. Our mutual friends have picked up on this too, but I don't get the sense that Sarah minds it. I make no further references to Simon for the rest of the evening and by the end of a shared bottle of cheap white wine I'm sure that Sarah has forgotten all about him.

Most of the rest of the week passes unremarkably enough – he is there the next day, same chair, same side-on sitting position, same easy smile. We exchange greetings as I pass his chair and sit near the back of the room, half expecting that he'll turn his head again and smile and I can feel myself preening, arranging my hair and top to hang just right, holding my head high ready to meet that gaze with a smile of my own, but the turn of the head doesn't come – he sits there, smiling, turning down politely all offers for a different chair, or to sit straight, again seemingly paying no attention at all to what is going on around him. Once or twice, I think that I almost catch him looking at me, but that he has just turned away before I can catch his eye. I start telling myself that I am just being ridiculous and by the middle of Thursday I have convinced myself that there was absolutely nothing in Monday's exchange and that I should pull myself together a bit. I can remember managing to make myself feel quite cross at him for Monday's performance, clearly he's some sort of odd fantasist who gave me his attention for five minutes whilst he started imagining what it must be like to be with me – and look at him, he can't even sit in a chair straight. I make sure that every evening when I go back to the flat, I don't mention him to Sarah again, and she seems to have forgotten all about him anyway. She is certainly good enough that she doesn't mention him when Ben comes over and spends the night a couple of times and the three of us share takeaway food and cheap wine and watch a cheap DVD and laugh and talk.

By Friday I am thoroughly bored with the whole process, the sitting around listening to people who are clearly enamoured with their own subjects (the infection control lady seemed fit to burst with her enthusiasm for dirty mattresses "you MUST, simply MUST unzip the covers"), drinking poor quality coffee from a vending machine (the hospital not even providing coffee) and making small talk with people you'll never work with and probably never see again in a hospital this size. This morning there was a definite lack of enthusiasm in getting ready and my jeans and jumper combo reflect that in spades – I haven't done anything with my hair except put it up in a ponytail and I have hardly any make up on.

Throughout the week we have had a selection of people and presenters, but there has been one guy who has clearly been tasked with keeping the days going and as best as possible to time. He comes in between sessions, has delivered a couple of talks himself and seems keen to learn everyone's name. He has been one of the ones that has tried to get that annoying dickhead to sit straight is his chair, with no success. Obviously, by Friday he has had enough.

"Don't you think it's particularly rude and disrespectful to sit like that?" he says.

"No, not at all", Simon replies in good humour.

"Well, you're clearly not paying attention to a single thing that is being said and having spent the whole week lolling there like some petulant teenager", he says, rather more loudly than I think he intended.

Hah – that told you, I think.

"I can assure you," says Simon, in no less a calm and friendly manner than if he had been asked for a cup of tea, "that you have my complete attention."

"So, what have I just been saying?" says the presenter, slightly louder again. The room has gone quiet, and I can see people shuffling uncomfortably in their seats at this exchange.

Very calmly, and still in the exact same, easy pleasant manner, Simon meets the presenter's level gaze, and then repeats almost verbatim the last few minutes of the presentation. He doesn't look at a piece of paper, or as far as I can tell the projection on the wall of the latest slide. He summarises the previous line of discussion and then summarises the lectures so far today.

The lecturer doesn't know what to say or do, and it's clear from his stance.

After a few seconds silence, he lamely concludes by "Good…well….", and then carries on with the remainder of his bit.

Hah – that told you, I think, and then mentally kick myself.

All week he has never spoken until spoken to, asked no questions and not volunteered any opinions, never challenged, and barely spoken to anyone else in the room. Some people cannot help themselves but to have an opinion on everything and ask a series of increasingly ridiculous questions on an increasingly unrelated set of subjects, and I can't think of anyone else that hasn't pitched in at some point, even me – the guy running things has been keen to get everyone involved at some point – but without any attempt to be rude or to be anything else other than, well, charming, I suppose, Simon has politely rebuffed such efforts, or, politely, answered the questions flawlessly with no hint of condescension.

At break times, whilst others gather in small groups by the coffee machine or the vending machine and talk about banalities, he is nowhere to be seen – and I find myself wondering where it is that he goes. I don't actively look for him or try and follow him or anything – I think that would be insane – but whenever I do a quick scan of the break area, he is not there, whilst I am stuck standing around drinking terrible coffee and listening to the latest news on 'what the weather might be like tomorrow' or 'I've got children – and aren't I interesting as a result'.

The group parts company at about 3.30 and there's a few goodbyes and see-you-around and we-must-keep-in-touch. I leave the room before he does and stop outside to get my coat on – whilst I'm doing so, he walks up alongside me silently, takes my elbow in his hand and simply says "Nice to meet you, Dee, hopefully I'll see you again."

And he is gone.

I stand there feeling like someone has dumped ice water down my spine whilst simultaneously setting my elbow on fire and watch him go. He does not look back.

Feeling totally shell shocked I pull myself together enough to go home, although later that evening I can't even remember the journey.

I think about him from time to time over the next week and wonder where he is – sometimes I kick myself for not finding out where he would be working, and other times I congratulate myself for the same reason – he is clearly a man with issues, I tell myself. I start working in the Haematology lab, meet my colleagues, get used to the environment and being in a job, and I think about him less and less. I don't think that I'll ever see him again.

Ella

It is almost three weeks later that I am trudging up the long track to the vineyard. I am tired, footsore and feel grubby, but I am finally here. I have quite a bit more money left than I thought I would have which is probably down in part to overestimating how much things would cost and saving money at every opportunity – walking as much as possible, eating as little as possible, travelling by bus overnight so that I can sleep on the bus rather than in a hostel. It is cold, colder than it was at the farm which surprises me – I expected it to be sunny and warm whereas the reality is that it's a bit grey and a bit damp. I got off the overnight coach in Dijon whilst it was barely light and have walked the fifteen or so miles this morning waiting for the sun to break through which it has so far failed to do.

The journey from home has been tiring but not particularly eventful – some people have tried making conversation on buses and in cafes and on the street, and between Polish, French and a smattering of English and German I have been able to get by – if there's one thing I would say about myself it's that I have a gift for languages.

I did have some trouble in Berlin though. Berlin itself was a beautiful city, and I was not at all disappointed to have a few hours between connecting buses wandering and spending a little money on a small coffee. It was bright and cold and lovely. I took my coffee and sat in Potsdamer Platz, sitting on a bench reading one of my books and just enjoying being for a moment, killing time until making my next connection, when a shadow fell across my book, and I looked up to see four German boys surrounding me. One sat beside me and starting talking about him and his friends taking me for a drink, then if I was looking for a place to stay for the night coming back to the flat they supposedly all shared, and generally tried to make a nuisance of himself but I pretended not to understand a word of what he was saying – when he went to put an arm around my shoulder I hit it hard with the book, much to the amusement of his friends, and they eventually got bored and went away. I don't imagine that that was all that they were offering. "Let the little bitch freeze if she wants," I heard one of them say as they went away. It took me a good twenty minutes after they left to stop shaking and headed off in the opposite direction to the one that they had left in. The circuitous route back to Charlottenburg meant that I was later for the bus than I had planned to be, and I climbed on to the back of the coach with some relief.

My little bag seems to have got heavier as the journey has gone on, but I have no regrets for bringing my books – not least because of Berlin – because they have been a great comfort and company to me at times, old friends that I have been grateful to have along on the journey with me.

I am almost up the vineyard house – I can clearly see the bright curtains in the windows, a sure sign I am in the right place. I am smiling to myself about this when the door flies open and an apparition trailing flowing clothes and a shawl and carrying a large blanket rushes out to greet me.

"Oh, my little Lebski, little Lebski, thank God you're safe and ALIVE!" she says, wrapping me in the blanket and hugging me tighter than I think I have ever been hugged before. I haven't even had chance to put down my case or raise my arms and now feel almost mummified by this big blanket and the woman trying very hard to change my alive status by hugging me to death, it seems. She's sobbing onto my shoulder, and I have to say that the whole thing really does take me by surprise. She stands back for a moment holding me by the shoulders and there are real tears down her face. This is the first of only the two times I have ever seen Sabine cry.

She bustles me into the house, telling me about how worried she and Olek have been, how terrified they were when Mama called to say that I had gone missing, how everyone had become convinced I had been kidnapped, or murdered or done away with somehow. How for days Mama and she were waiting by the phone for any piece of news, any - even if it were a call from the police to recount the worst, and now here I am, safe and well. She must call Mama to let know.

"No," I say firmly. "No, don't. She will only want me to go back, and I am not going to go."

"But my little Lebski you must!" she says, "It's your home!"

"Did everybody miss me?" I say.

The question hangs in the air for a moment and that is all I need to see the answer.

Tiredness has made me irritable, and I say something that I immediately regret to make the point.

"Did Uncle Olek go back home?" I say. And although I regret saying it, I can see that Sabine understands. A moment of silence passes between us before she leaps up.

"Of course! Olek! – Anna?" she calls. A woman in her twenties appears, presumably Anna and before she has chance to speak Sabine tells her in faultless French to go and find Olek and bring him to the house as quickly as possible. Anna looks at me, nods her head once and rushes off.

Sabine insists that I have a bath, telling me that Olek could be anywhere, and it will probably take Anna a while to find him. She also insists that she come and help me bathe, and whilst at first, I try and refuse I am too tired to argue about it and agree. I end up sitting in their huge, enamelled bath whilst Sabine vigorously sponges everything, my hair, my back, my limbs, my face, before wordlessly handing me the sponge and meaningfully nodding toward my lap. She turns her back whilst I take care of my personal care, but all the time she is talking constantly – how the vineyard is doing, where she and Olek have been, the gossip in the town about people I don't know and am unlikely to ever meet. She tuts loudly when she is washing my feet at the broken and now hardened skin and part-healed blisters with a scolding look that can only be described as motherly.

The water is lovely and hot, and has a beautiful fragrance from some bath oil Sabine poured in. I can feel an ache that had been there so long I had forgotten that I had it leave my body and despite the constant talking, I almost drift off once or twice. Sabine talks constantly, switching with ease between Polish and French but with a speed that makes it hard for me to keep up at times.

It is one of the most blissful experiences of my life.

She even towels me down afterwards and hands me one of her own bath robes – far too big for my slight frame, but thick and warm and luxuriant, before bustling me into what must be the spare room and putting me into bed. It can be no later than about 10am but I suddenly feel more tired than I have ever done and fall into a deep and dreamless sleep.

When I awake it is already becoming dark outside and my stomach is rumbling for a change. I can hear voices downstairs, but they sound friendly, calm even. There is a large glass of what turns out to be grape juice on the bedside table and I drink more than half of it in one go. I am still in Sabine's robe, so I get myself up, tidy up the robe so that it looks more presentable, slip my feet into the sheepskin lined slippers that have also miraculously appeared and pad downstairs holding my juice.

The vineyard house is quite old and the wooden floors squeak and groan as I walk, so it is no surprise that I am barely halfway down the stairs before Sabine and Olek appear at the bottom, smiling up at me. Olek looks a lot older and more tired than I have ever seen him and I wonder if there have been tears from him too, but I don't stare and I don't ask. Sabine throws herself at me again and tells me that I look much more like her little Lebski than I did when I arrived. She kisses me on both cheeks and seems almost reluctant to let me go when Olek goes to put an arm around me, so he ends up awkwardly holding us both. He smells of sweat which make my nose wrinkle a little when he kisses me on both cheeks, and they usher me into the kitchen. I have smelled the stew from the hallway and my grumbling stomach must be so loud that they both can hear it. I am guided into a chair at their huge kitchen table whilst Anna ladles a large portion of beef stew and places what looks like a whole loaf of bread on a plate for me. There is a glass of red wine there too, along with two others, one empty apart from a few dregs and one half full.

"We're so pleased you're safe," Olek says, "that we opened one of the '84's to celebrate."

I have never been much of a drinker as father rarely allowed wine in the house. The few experiences I have of alcohol are when father allowed a bottle or two for a special occasion or when father had made a particularly good cider that he would want to show off, and even then, my wine would be diluted with water before I could have it.

This wine is warming and luscious – it smells of berries and summer and tastes like I am drinking warm red velvet. That and the hearty stew are doing wonders for me.

Anna makes herself absent whilst Sabine and Olek want to know everything from when I left Lutynia almost three weeks ago to now. I tell them what I can missing out Tomasz' part in it all and the brief encounter with the German boys in Berlin. I tell them that I walked a lot, which I did, and that I slept somewhere safe every night, which I didn't. I don't tell them about my little stash of money or how I got it, and by the end they have a picture of a 17-year-old girl hitching almost all the way from Wroclaw to Dijon which isn't that far from the truth.

"You must let us tell your mother, Ella," says Sabine. "She has been going out of her mind with worry." I am feeling less antagonistic now that I have slept, eaten and had another glass of that delicious red wine and we agree that Mama should know that I am alive and safe, but not where I am nor who I am with. I remain adamant about keeping my father out of this and insist that if we speak to Mama, we are to tell her to keep it to herself.

In the end it's Sabine who calls her that night. We have moved from the kitchen, which as every person who has ever lived on a farm will tell you is the where almost all business of any kind is conducted, through to a low-ceilinged sitting room with a large comfortable looking sofa and two matching armchairs that are either side of a fireplace. I initially ducked as I entered the room but can just about stand up straight without cracking my head on a beam. It seems Every surface is covered with colourful fabrics – including the arms and backs of the furniture – and Sabine arranges herself carefully on an armchair next to a side tale with both a coloured glass lamp and a telephone on it.

"Kaja," she says, "I want you to know that God has answered your prayers and kept Ella safe for us". I can hear my mother sobbing from the other side of the room to where Sabine is sitting. "No, she didn't tell me where she was, but she said she was safe and had a roof over her head. She said she's sorry that she couldn't tell you and she couldn't call you, and that there are some things a mother and only a mother should know." The stress on the word 'only' is apparent from here. I can't hear Mama's side of the conversation but it's clear from Sabine's that Mama understands what she is being told. "No, I told you, she wouldn't tell me where she is, but I am certain that she has a place to stay and people to take care of her." With this, she looks up at me and nods slightly, and Olek appears from behind me, places a hand on my shoulder and gives it a gentle squeeze. "She promised to call me again soon," she says, "and I will persuade her to give you a call too," she says pointedly looking at me. I look up at Olek and he nods gently at me – I nod slightly and bow my head a little. "Yes, I'm sure she'll call soon. Sleep well, Kaja, Olek and I both send our love."

We talk some more into the night, Olek raising a fire in the hearth whilst Sabine asks patient questions to fill in gaps in the history of the last three weeks, which I fill with as near to the truth as is plausible or suitable for them to hear. Neither of them asks why I left, neither of them asks why I came here. By ten o'clock I can feel my eyelids closing again and Sabine packs me off to bed again, this time with a set of her cotton pyjamas and a stone hot water bottle. I bid Sabine goodnight as she strokes my hair, she kisses me on the forehead and hear her footsteps creaking down the stairs. Before long, sleep is upon me again.

Alina

It's sex that's the worst. I can put up with the silences, the shouting, the pushing, the ranting, and the raving. I can put up with how he speaks to me, to Christiana and to my mother, I can put up with sitting on my daughter's bed rocking her to sleep because he is drunk and angry again. I can even put up with the occasional careless slap across the face because I said something out of turn or didn't have something just right when he got home, but every time I have sex with my husband, or more accurately whenever he has sex with me, I feel sickened afterwards. I am completely repulsed by him, by his body, by his attitude and I feel physically sick every time he touches me. It is all I can do not to lie there crying every time, his enormous bulk bearing down on me, grinding away at me. It's never been a particularly fulfilling experience for me, but it has got worse and worse.

I can't right now think of a good reason why I married him – I knew he was trouble from the start. I was only twenty when he started courting me and perhaps at thirty-five, he seemed like a worldly wise older man with a bit of a wild side. I really can't remember why I agreed to go out with him, let alone marry him.

I can remember wanting to get away from home as soon as possible. Andrei is much like my father – rash, bold, drunkard, violent – and perhaps by going with him I was, how do you say, jumping out of the pan into the fire? That was probably it – in my rush to get away from one terrible man I ran straight into the arms of another.

Of course, I had had plenty of attention from boys and men – I am slim and attractive, and learning ballet for many years has given me a toned body, although it is an unending regret that I have never been tall enough to perform in anything other than an amateur capacity – so at twenty I felt like I knew, or at least thought I knew, what life, love and marriage was about. Married at twenty-one, pregnant at twenty-two. And so now, like my mother, I keep my head down, look out for my daughter.

He was attractive back then – he had had a muscular frame; he played a lot of sport and went to the gym at least twice a week. He seemed caring and attentive, brought me flowers from time to time, and treated me like a princess. I felt like this was the love you read about in fairy tales, saved from a terrible life to be rescued by a handsome and generous prince, to be carried off on a white horse. I told him I loved him often and drew hearts around our names and told him how happy I was to be married to a man like him. He became the centre of my world and once we were married, I was determined to do whatever I could to please my husband. My husband! Just saying those words gave me such pleasure.

What I have realised though is that this was just my naivety telling me the stories I needed to hear which fitted in with him wanting to own me, wanting to possess me and all the flowers and presents were him pretending to be a better person than he was – not a prince, not even a knave, but a dark and consuming creature. Even back then I saw flashes of the man he was when I'd turn him down for a date or to go back to his house, and I must have made excuses for him in my own head.

What a fool I was. Now he is forty-six, the body and fitness have dissolved into this round, pale, sweaty lump and I have lived with the real Andrei for nearly ten years – the veil dropped almost as soon as mine was put away. Christiana is the one thing that keeps me going – my beautiful, beautiful daughter. I take care of her and sleep in her bed with her when times are bad and I stroke her hair and I read her stories and I tell her that it will all be all right, when in my heart I can only hope that it will be.

Then I will have to stomach him bending me into the positions he wants, making me dress in the way that he wants then grinding away me, or pushing my head down into his lap or pushing me onto my hands and knees so that he can…so he can have me in other ways.

At least like that he can't see the tears if they come.

And once he's finished with me, he's lost interest – he wants to go back to his beer or wine or vodka, or back to his computer games or videos and as long as I am out of his sight, he doesn't care what I do. That's when I can take myself to our bed in some ridiculous outfit he's made me wear, or Christiana's bed, and let out the tears that I won't let him see.

When he brought me to England it was because I could earn more money here than I could as a nurse in Romania. I could not speak a word of English, Christiana was only six, but that was his big plan, move to England to make a fortune for himself. I don't think it was a coincidence that at the time he decided to make his fortune in England he was wanted in connection with the hospitalisation of a man in our local bar, which wouldn't have been the first time he had been in trouble with the police, or in prison either – by the time he met me he had already had a prison sentence, something that I wasn't to learn about until much later, and then only during some drunken abuse and threat about what would happen to me if I didn't do what he wanted.

I had to start out by working as a nursing assistant, even though I was a qualified nurse, because the language barrier meant that I could not communicate properly at all with the English people. After a while though, I had learned enough that I could do the exams I needed to in English to have my registration and to work as a nurse. I am proud of being a nurse, helping people who need help, and I think I do a fairly good job of it too. I am efficient and work hard and I know what is right and what is wrong – it upsets people when I tell them that they are doing something wrong, but I don't care. I am not free though; I have no friends at work and all of my money goes straight into his bank account to pay for his new car or his nights out. At least he paid for Mama to come and live with us, but only so that she can look after Christiana when I am working so that he doesn't have to or to pay for someone else to.

So, I live from home to work, work to home – I work three nursing jobs to keep the money coming in – and I can even put up with this too.

One of the jobs is a long stay elderly medical ward – the patients are nice enough in the most part, some of them end up staying for very long periods of time and I can get to know them and their families, which is nice, but the other staff don't seem to think that it is worth their time or effort to look after these people properly. I can see them, outside the fire escape door, still in their uniforms smoking and laughing, whilst people in beds wait to have the simple pleasures like a bath or a shave, or sometimes even the opportunity to go to the toilet. There are little groups that each have their own little leader, and the ward's maintenance man seems to be maintaining a post by the front desk drinking tea and chatting to all the visitors as they come in. They all think he's wonderful, but I can see him for what he is, a lazy, fat, two faced liar. Yes, he is all lovely to your face but the minute your back is turned he will be telling anyone that will listen about why you're not right for this job, or how that visitor shouldn't dress like that, where does she think she is, and why don't the management do something about the heating, or the lighting, or the immigrants or number of visitors per bed. He is always willing to stir up trouble, that one.

The manager, Alice, is a lovely lady but really is not cut out for this if you ask me. She has let all these staff act how they want and will not challenge them, tell them off, or drag them out of their little groups. Instead, she works all around the clock trying to make sure that everyone at least gets the basic care covered, it is not unusual to see her here long after the rest of the staff have gone home, filling out charts, doing medicines and caring for patients.

I work at a care home as well and then work for an agency filling in extra nursing shifts whenever I can. It is tiring working all these hours but for every hour I am at work, it is not an hour that I have to spend at home keeping out of the way or having sex. At work, instead of being Andrei's wife, I can be Staff Nurse Alina, taking care of people in the best way I know how.

It is my release that in truth is no release at all – but at least it is better than the alternative.

Do not misunderstand me, I know that a wife's place is to do her husband's bidding, and Andrei reminds me of that frequently. "Behave yourself," he will say, "or I'll throw you out – I could find another three like you on the nearest street corner." I don't doubt that he would throw me out, either – and then I won't be able to take care of Christiana any more and keep her from the worst of him. So, like a wife and a mother should, I do what I am bid, and I put up with Andrei and I put up with the sex, but I really wish I didn't have to.

Dee

A great deal can happen in almost two years. For example, I have been working steadily and have been told that I am in line for getting a promotion to manage the haematological services attached to the hospital's Emergency Department – never mind the prestige, I can really do with the salary bump.

Ben got himself a job too, and I moved out of the flat share so that we could live together. It is not much, it is a one bedroomed place nearer to the east end of London than I'd like, and we overlook a flyover – but at least it's ours. And as Ben and I promised to each other, we are planning the wedding.

Sarah met a nice West Indian man that her Mum would approve of, and I even managed to persuade her to come and work here with me, so although we don't live together anymore, I still see her pretty much every day – although we're both working there's days when it still feels like we're at Uni together and we laugh and joke and get too drunk on nights out.

When I get told that I am getting the senior position I am ecstatic and relieved – at least there is going to be some more money for the wedding pot. My Mother and Father have been helping out with things as they can and Mother, being Mother, wants to be involved in every detail of planning. It is not every day her only daughter gets married, so I keep being told. I really don't mind, it's nice to see so much of them, especially as I hardly get the chance to go back to Bristol - working five days a week and partying for at least two days a week takes its toll on both your time and your finances.

The transition to the new post is easy enough – finish on Friday doing lab work, start on Monday in a different lab, still doing lab work but overseeing the work of two others, Samantha and Dilip. I still have the same job title on my badge, but I make a mental note to get it changed to Senior Laboratory Assistant as soon as I can. Dilip gives me the guided tour as such – there's the blood fridges, there's the centrifuge, there's the door...which must take all of three minutes. Then he shows me round to the ED and introduces me to a few of the doctors there. They all seem nice enough and welcoming. He takes me through to the resuscitation area so that I can have a little look – I might be asked to come in there during major traumas, he explains, if the staff can't leave to fetch blood or bring samples themselves.

I am standing in the doorway looking around the place and Dilip is talking about some of the recent cases they have had through here when I see him – he steps out from behind a wheeled screen and starts to turn toward me. I'm fairly sure that I stop breathing and it feels like everything is in slow motion as I see him turn his head, catch sight of me and his smile spreads across his face – he alters the direction he was heading and comes straight toward me.

"Dee!" he cries, as though I am a long-lost friend, "how on earth are you? It's lovely to see you!"

He encircles me in a huge hug that almost lifts me off the ground. He is taller than I remember, and much broader of shoulder than I had expected – I hadn't seen him in anything but a nondescript shirt or a jumper before and here he is in a short-sleeved tunic, with his long and powerful arms around me. Before I know what I am doing I am hugging him back, my head against his chest and my stomach doing somersaults.

"Oh, err, hi Simon" Dilip is saying, "this is Deni...."

"Yes, yes, yes, thanks Dil, I know Dee!" he roars jovially. He is still hugging me, and I haven't attempted to let go yet, even though my feet are barely touching the floor. I can hear his voice through his chest as I stand here. "Come on," he says to me, "let me introduce you to the gang. I'll bring her back by midnight" he says to Dilip with a wink, and then we are off.

He leads me off by the hand like a schoolchild, introducing me to people and showing various pieces of gadgetry like an excited child himself. Everyone we stop and speak to he has some sort of biography to reveal – "Tom, this is Dee, and Dee, this is Tom – Tom played flank forward at university and I am trying to persuade him to lace his boots up again. What do you say, Tom? Play one half?" or "Angela, this is my good friend Dee, and Dee this is Angela, she took me under her wing when I started, couldn't have been a nicer person to show me the ropes!" or "Laura, this is Dee and Dee, this is Laura, no, sorry, the *lovely* Laura, if I were twenty years older and she weren't already married I'd snap her up!" – everyone has a tale added to their introduction and no one has anything but a smile or a laugh for what Simon has to say. I feel almost dizzy rushing from person to person being bombarded with information about their hobbies, their families, or some other random facts about them. No one is missed out, either – even the man changing the bins gets an introduction.

We seem to be back in the main area again, and he spreads his arms wide and says, "So, what do you think? This is my domain! None may enter, save by my leave!" He is smiling down at me, and I really don't know what to say.

"So, this is where you work?" is the lame result.

"Yes, worked emergency for nearly fifteen years, man and boy. Wouldn't want to work anywhere else! So, you've come to help out the lab boys, have you?"

"No, well, yes, I'm the new senior lab assistant."

"Excellent!" he beams, "that means I'll be able to drop in on you any time!"

Dilip is hanging around looking like a cross between really, really anxious and mildly put out. In the absence of anything clever to say I give him another hug – which I am pleased to say gets returned – and I leave with Dilip promising that we will catch up properly another time.

Much to my disappointment, that is it – that is pretty much how it stays for months despite my efforts to visit the department much more often than is strictly necessary – for example, checking on the blood warming machine, checking on their stocks of transfusion sets and phlebotomy equipment. Anyone who knows anything about hospitals will know that there are about five people who will check on an Emergency Department's stock levels, on their machines, and equipment, so it certainly isn't the senior lab assistant's job.

Likewise, I find that I am volunteering to 'help out' if there is a major trauma in by fetching and carrying blood samples and units for transfusion. Fortunately, my boss and the rest of the department see this as me being super keen to impress and be helpful. I never know when he'll be there as they all work shift work, so before I know it, I find myself volunteering to be on-call for the department and going round there late at night "just to check" if there's anything needed before I retire to the on-call room.

I am rewarded from time to time because I'll walk in and there he is – he always seems to be surrounded by people, whether it's other staff or patients or relatives, and he seems to treat each as serenely and benevolently as he does everyone else. He always has the same easy smile that leaves me wondering how he manages it – sometimes I think it would be hard enough to keep your own sanity, never mind a constant smile and constant patience working here.

But he does always make time and space for me – he always smiles when he sees me, and if he can't leave what he's doing there and then I know he'll make sure he comes over to me as soon as he can. One day I walked into the resuscitation room to see him up to the elbow in some guy's chest, with blood and panic everywhere – when he looked up and saw me, he just smiled and winked at me and carried on. If you were to ask me about him 'totally unflappable' would go a long way to describing him.

If he is there, I always know that sooner or later he'll come and ask me how I am, put his arms around me and hold me – and every time he does, I feel like I fit perfectly, just there, being held. I can't stop myself from putting my arms around him and holding him back – and it's always me that holds on the longest, I don't want it to end.

No one in his department seems to mind this behaviour at all – on the rare occasions that anyone says something, he'll always say that we've known each other forever and that seems to be that. But eventually Sarah gets to hear about my volunteer on call and my 'enthusiasm' for helping out in the emergency department. We are on one of our regular nights out when she just comes out with it.

"So, are you sleeping with him yet?" she says.

"What?? Who???" I splutter into my cosmo.

"That guy, Simon. You've not shut up about him for months."

I think that this is something of an exaggeration – I might have mentioned this or that happened but not shutting up about him I don't agree with. I tell her so, too, preceded by a loud "Fuck off!"

"Uh huh," she says, and I get the Pirate Look from her which always makes me wither a bit, "and do you tell Ben all the same stories that you're telling me?"

"Of course I do!" I reply hotly – this is often how I speak to Sarah when I am telling her a bare faced lie and even though I am certain that she knows this I do it anyway.

"I'm surprised he hasn't been down there and taken a look at this guy himself then – if I was him, I'd want to see who is making my future wife dance around like she's got hot pennies in her shoes and keeping her away all night for on-call. That she doesn't need to do" she adds pointedly.

I'm on my fifth cosmo by this time and I embark on an ill-advised opening up of what I think about him – I admit that I like him, that I have never met anyone quite like him, that he always makes time for me ("but that's how he is with everyone" I add helpfully) and I foolishly tell her about how I feel like I fit whenever he holds me. I also relate to her (for probably the hundredth time) the story of that induction day and what a terrible person he must be.

"Go very careful, Denise" – she only calls me Denise when she's being very serious, and her West Indian accent adds gravitas – "you sound like you are at risk of losing yourself. You haven't forgotten that you're getting married in three months' time, have you?"

"Of course I haven't – and anyway, it's not like we've ever done anything else other than have the occasional hug and he never says anything to suggest he likes me other than tell me it's good to see me."

It is during this conversation that I have the realisation of the truth of this bare bones, five cosmo assessment – he has never given me any indication of what he thinks about me or whether he likes me at all. I realise that we have never talked about anything at all – I don't know if he's married, or living with someone, or gay. What if he is gay? Maybe the friendliness with everyone is because he is friendly with everyone? Maybe I am nothing special to him at all? Maybe he is gay? Then I remember the induction again and think he is probably not that friendly with everyone, anyway, and begin to think I am caught up in some big act.

Sarah has never been one not to notice my moods and my face must have fallen so far that I must look like my chin is on the floor. Suddenly she is holding me, and I feel very silly and childish for having made such an obvious fool of myself. I am such a fool sometimes.

Another cosmo or two later and the last I can clearly remember from that night is Sarah and me dancing somewhat expansively to a disco track that was red-hot something like twenty years ago. I have to rely on Sarah to fill in the blanks later, and she takes much delight in filling me in with graphic detail about copious pink vomit over London Bridge.

Ella

I feel no pressure from Sabine or Olek to do anything at all for the whole time I stay with them. Sabine is like a big sister and a mother all rolled together, and Olek just seems happy to see me happy. As I promised Sabine I would I spoke to Mama and told her that I was all right, and I've phoned her a couple of more times since too. Although she probably knows where I am she hasn't let on that she knows and hasn't made me tell her. Sabine promises me faithfully that she hasn't said anything, and I believe her.

Olek shows me around the vineyard, and Sabine and I take long walks around the place – Olek is producing a fine grape, so I am told, and the vineyard is doing well. Certainly, Sabine always seems to be able to afford the latest in fashionable clothes, provided they tend toward the flowing and lightweight style. I have never seen someone with quite such a selection of jewellery, even though she insists that there is not much that she has of great value, it is impressive, nonetheless.

I have been with them since the beginning of spring and all through the summer and although neither of them have said a word about it, I start to feel like I should contribute something towards my being here. More than that, though, the inactivity is taking its toll – I have definitely put on weight and although Sabine insists that I am still skinny for my height I am feeling sluggish and fat.

Over the weeks I have really got to know Anna too – my first guess was right, she turned out to be twenty-one, the daughter of another vineyard owner from further south who happens to be a friend of Olek's. Anna has been with them for almost three years keeping house which depending on who you listen to was either as a favour to her father or her first step to exploring the world. She has her own annexe at the vineyard, nothing special except for her own bedroom and bathroom and a tiny lounge area where she and I have had the occasional chat, giggle and glass of Olek's latest produce – we're close enough in age that we can talk about clothes and music and dreams well enough, and although she doesn't speak a word of Polish I have been able to get by on my French which has improved dramatically. Olek will sometimes come into the kitchen at the house to find Sabine, Anna and I in either a heated discussion about something (usually fashion) or laughing with each other over something ridiculous (usually fashion) and chatting away in French. Olek, barely speaking more than a few words of French, invariably will shake his head and walk out again, much to the amusement of the three of us.

The other advantage of spending time with Anna is that having been here a while now she has friends in the town that she introduces me to and knows all the best bars around that are in the price range of a couple of farm girls, as she describes us. I don't have any money apart from what was left over from my travel budget, but she is always able to get a couple of men to buy us a drink or two on the few occasions we have gone out together. Invariably I spend the night sipping on a small beer in some quiet corner whilst Anna holds men in thrall or dances with her friends, but she makes time to come and sit with me and chat – I feel like I am under her wing sometimes, but really, I am quite happy to just be out and enjoying the atmosphere.

It is Anna that suggests to me that I might make a good au pair for someone from the town. When she suggests it at first, I dismiss it, but once I give it a little thought, I can see the merit in the idea. When we talk it over with Sabine, she immediately thinks it's a wonderful idea and happens to know *just* the couple who might be after someone to look after their little one whilst they work, and before long I get to meet Gabrielle and Felix and their one-year-old little girl called Diane.

It's not particularly trying work and I would have done it for nothing just to get me out of the house, but the three days a week looking after Diane and perhaps doing a bit of housekeeping earns me a few francs that I can then give to Olek (much to the mortification of Sabine who refuses to take a single centime) and still have some left so that I can buy myself a few clothes and buy my own small beer when Anna and I go out in the town. It is not far into the town and I usually walk in to arrive on Gabrielle and Felix's doorstep for 8:30am, spend the day playing games or reading or going out for walks with Diane until around four thirty when Gabrielle gets home. I know that Gabrielle only has a half day on a Friday, and uses the extra time to meet up with friends or perhaps just have a coffee on her own, and I don't begrudge her that at all – she is always grateful to me for having taken care of Diane and always pays me a little more than we agreed (especially if the visit with friends has been to a bar) and then I'll walk home again.

Sometimes, at times like this when I am recalling the time, I reflect that it was funny how quickly that I had come to think of the vineyard as home.

I am at the park one day in November watching Diane throw some old bread to the ducks on the pond when I see someone that I think I recognise – I notice him mostly because he seems to be spending a lot of time staring at me from the café where he and another man are sitting and talking. He is beginning to make me feel uncomfortable, both because of the staring and because he looks familiar and I just cannot place him – twenties, black jacket, black hair, black shirt with some sort of motif on the front that I cannot see properly, a bit Goth looking. Eventually he says something to his companion and gets up to walk over to me.

"Ella?" he says.

"Yes?"

"Hi, I thought that was you – it's Sepp, we met a couple of weeks ago at the Old Lion? You were out with your sister, Anna?"

He probably did meet me, but I don't remember him clearly, and Anna will sometimes introduce me as her sister to save explanations – although what people think of a Polish speaking sister of a French girl, I have no idea.

"Hi, yeah, Sepp – nice to see you again, what are you doing here?"

"Oh, I'm just out for a coffee with a friend from work, we're sat just over there, would you like to join us?"

"No, I can't – I'm working myself" I say, pointing to Diane, "I have that little one to look after."

"Yours?" he says, looking a bit shocked.

"NO!" I laugh, "I look after her a few days a week, you know, so that her Mum and Dad can go to work" – he looks almost relieved.

At that the conversation grinds awkwardly to a halt, so I say "Well, I must go, I'll need to get this one a snack and a nap before her Mum comes home. Nice to see you again."

I turn to leave and have got halfway to Diane before he calls out.

"Wait! Wait!" he says, and jogs over to where I am now standing, "How would you like to go out for a drink sometime?"

"Sure, we'll keep a look out for you next time we go out," I say.

"No, I mean, you know, just you and me."

I make a show of thinking about this a little, which I am. He is not bad looking but I can't think why he'd be interested in me, I'm a good six inches taller than he is but from the look of the size of his arms probably less than half his weight.

"Sure, OK" I say, a little embarrassed, and turn to head back to Diane.

"Wait!" he calls again, "Can I have your number?"

I think about this and pull out the paperback I have in my pocket, carefully tear out a blank page from the back and write down the telephone number of the house. I press it into his hand, and I am across to pick up Diane and carry her on my hip rather than try to get her into the pushchair whilst he is still watching me – I can't imagine having that struggle with my own audience. I scurry off without a glance backwards.

"Thank you!!" he calls out to my retreating back.

I give Sepp almost no thought at all except to think that he will probably think twice about calling or that it was some mistake or a plan to get closer to Anna – who is by anyone's estimate much more beautiful than I am – and get back to Gabrielle and Felix's house in good time. Gabrielle gets home earlier than usual – I am guessing no social appointments today – so I am back at the vineyard much earlier than usual too. Sabine is sitting at the kitchen table with an unreadable expression on her face when I walk in, and even Anna turns away and busies herself with the stove as I sit down.

"Everything OK?" I ask.

"Fine, fine….er, fine" says Sabine, "Good day, was it? You're home early?"

Her voice seems…odd, somehow. Not angry, not happy, strained almost.

I tell her the most exciting parts about looking after an almost two-year-old, which is to say not much, and leave it at that.

"Only…." she starts, pauses, and then plunges on "There was a call for you. From someone called Sepp. He said you knew each other but wouldn't say why he was calling. Do you know someone called Sepp?"

At the mention of the name, I think I can hear Anna drawing a deep breath which she seems to hold for an unnaturally long length of time.

"Yes, Anna and I met him in a bar the other day and I saw him again today when I was out in the park. He asked me out."

Anna seems to have stopped breathing entirely now, and is on the verge of toppling over as she leans back to hear as much as she can.

"So, what's he like, this Sepp?"

"I don't really know – I didn't remember him from before, but he seemed to remember me and he came over to me in the park when I was out with Diane today. He seems nice enough" I add lamely.

"Well" …..pause….. "well, you're old enough to know what you're doing, I'm sure, just promise me you'll be careful" she concludes, before adding "And for God's sake don't tell Olek. Anna, how's that beef coming along?"

And that's it – we get on with dinner, Olek comes in from the vineyard and the four of us have dinner together with some freshly baked bread that Anna has made. I think I see Sabine cast an occasional glance in my direction over dinner, and once or twice in Anna's direction but nothing more is said. Anna asks me straight after dinner if I want to spend a bit of time in her annexe that evening for 'girl talk' and following a quick glance to Sabine to make sure that that is OK we go off together.

We are barely outside of the kitchen when Anna starts asking me lots of questions about Sepp, most of which I can't answer as I know almost nothing about him and can't even really remember what he looks like. Anna is astonished when I tell her this.

"But wasn't he the handsome one, you know the one that looks like he works out? Isn't that him?"

I tell her I have absolutely no idea whether that is him, and that I can't really be sure. I find myself struggling to recall what he looked like, but I am fairly sure about is that he is not the bodybuilder Anna is describing.

"So, are you going to call him back?" she says, smiling and nodding in encouragement.

"I haven't thought about it," I say, "I'll have a think about it."

"But you *are* going to call him back?!"

"Like I said, I'll have a think about it."

"I'll never understand you" she laughs "a handsome athlete asks you out and you have to think about. Sometimes I wonder if you're really my sister at all!"

We laugh about this and spend the evening talking about things like where we might go and what I should wear and whether or not he's got a friend so that Anna can come too. By the end of the evening, I have either decided (or been convinced, I am not sure which) that I will call him back, just to see and to satisfy Anna's own curiosity.

Alina

I barely have got know the woman, but it seems like I am the only one who is not surprised when the manager tells us in morning report that she is going to be leaving. There is much vocalised dismay at this and one or two of them even look like they could break out into tears at any second. I feel like slapping them in the face, it is not like the woman has announced she is dying, just that she has got another job that is nearer to her mother who is getting older and needs a bit of help in her old age. I have seen this woman working herself all hours of the day and night because the rest of these lazy staff have not been doing their jobs properly, and I cannot believe that it has taken this long for her to give up and move on. If I were her, I would be adding to my announcement that these lazy staff have caused her to leave, never mind her sick mother.

It is the only topic of conversation for the rest of the day, and from the sound of it the rest of their lives too. Considering the lack of support they gave her I can't understand why they seem so upset – there seems to be an unofficial contest for who can be the most upset or have the most inane reason for why she's leaving other than "we're too idle".

Not surprisingly the conversation starts to turn to who is going to replace her as the manager. One or two of them suggest other nurses who have been there for a while as next in line for the post – I find myself thinking that being highly unlikely as they are far too lazy to contemplate their own jobs, never mind taking on Alice's job as well and being responsible for the whole lot. The discussion turns through the day to considering that they are going to have to employ someone else from outside the hospital. It is whilst this debate goes on that I remember the stranger who visited about a month or so before – a tall man, must have been in his thirties, smartly dressed and looking for one of the directors. I let him onto the ward and called the director who was expecting him and took him off to some private meeting or other.

What made him stick in my mind was that a little later he and the director came back to the ward and had some sort of tour – he was looking at everything, the sluices, the equipment, the rotas, the office…. everything. I remember at the time thinking that he was some sort of auditor, but then why would an auditor take such an interest in the medical paperwork?

Now that the announcement has been made, I think that I have come up with the answer. I try to remember more about him – I remember his voice more than anything, clear and pleasant with a real English accent, not the English that the rest talk, but real English, spoken well. I remember his hands too; he shook my hand when he came back with the director – big and firm but not crushing as some men can be. And the smile – I remember that, he smiled a lot.

"You ain't saying much" says one of the care staff. This is not unusual for me; I don't get into discussions with the other staff, and I don't have either the time or the inclination to stand around chatting about my private life and trying to outdo anyone else with tales of misery. Sometimes I wonder if this is some strange English game – who can have the worst story or who can feel the worse about something.

"I don't have an opinion" I say "people work, they leave, some other people work, that's how it is. Always the work, sometimes different people but always the work."

I can tell from the looks on the faces that I am also expected to be crying or something for the loss of the manager, but I cannot help thinking that if she had managed better then she would not have needed to leave. I shrug my shoulders at them to indicate I have nothing more to say and they go off with sour looks on their sour faces. Obviously, I have upset some or all of them as for the rest of the day I cannot find anyone to help me with any dressings or bed changes or feeding but I have never been bothered by this and just get on with my work.

Brown eyes too, I think. Yes, brown eyes so dark that they are almost black, tall, and pleasantly spoken. I can't remember if there was a name and if there was what it was, and I don't share my thoughts with anyone else – the more I think about it the more I think that I have met the new manager already, but this is not a fact that I going to share with anyone.

Besides, if they had been in the ward when he came around, rather than standing around outside the fire exit, or having one of the twenty tea breaks they seem to need every day, they would have met him and made their own conclusions.

I don't often swear at all, but fuck them, I think. And smile to myself and get on with the rest of my day.

A little over a week later I think my suspicions are confirmed – I am on duty again when the same man comes to the ward to meet the same director. He is dressed in a similar fashion, suit and shirt and tie and I try to take in more of him without being too obvious that I am. Yes, brown eyes and short brown hair, going a little grey at the sides. Perhaps a little older than I first thought, but still thirties I would say. Broad shouldered, not slim but not fat either and he smiles a lot. I can't help feeling sorry for him right then – a smiling attitude is going to get you nowhere in this place, I think. These lazy staff will tear him to pieces, and he will be gone in less than a year, just like the last manager.

"Shame" I think to myself, and then wonder why.

Alice is here today as well and this man is introduced to those staff that are on duty as the man that it is taking her place – Simon Holcroft, and today is going to be his first day, having a period of handover from the outgoing manager. The two of them disappear off together for most of the morning, and unlike usual days the staff seem to go out of their way to make themselves busy or report things to the office. Usually, you can't get them to report anything – I have come on duty in the morning to find a dead patient in a bed from the night shift because the staff on duty 'didn't have time' to lay them out properly, none of the paperwork done, and the on-call doctor not even alerted. That was another job I did on my own because none of the staff had the time and were able to help me – or, if you believe my theory, none of the staff wanted to touch a dead person.

At lunch time they are both out of the office and Mr Holcroft is walking around the place introducing himself again, watching people work, asking questions and speaking to patients – but mostly he is watching, watching how people behave, where they go, what they are doing. He is clever this one, he is not making it obvious that what he really is doing is watching the staff rather than what he looks like he's doing which is making conversation and smiling at people. I am being as careful as I can not to let him know that I am watching him too, but it doesn't take him long to work out what I'm doing – he doesn't do anything about it or say anything, he just looks up from where he's talking to a patient straight to where he knows I am standing, looks directly at me whilst he carries on his conversation, smiles, then gives his full attention back to the patient in the bed.

It is a surprise that the old manager doesn't come in the next day and Mr Holcroft tells us that she has already left. There are a few shocked gasps at the announcement, and much gossiping in corners during the day, but otherwise little changes between today and yesterday – Mr Holcroft spends some time in the office and some time on the ward, walking, talking, chatting, and watching. The staff keep up their pretence of being hard workers, although this noticeably tails off as the week goes by. On the Friday afternoon he comes over to me and asks where everyone is – he says he feels like he is on the Marie Celeste, a reference I don't get until I look it up later, but I still smile politely at him as though I agree. When I do look it up, I remember thinking how appropriate that was – a ship under full sail with not a single soul on board, yes that is this place.

The following week it seems to be business as usual until the staff start getting letters in their pigeonholes with an appointment to go to Mr Holcroft's office to "meet the new manager and get to know each other". I am not surprised when this is greeted by scorn from almost everyone I hear talking about it, fear from most of the rest and a certain amount of rebellion along the lines of "I'm not going – I don't have anything that I want to talk to *him* about". I don't know how many do go, but I keep my appointment partly out of interest but mostly because he's my new boss and he has asked. Again, when we meet up, I can see what he is doing – he is sizing up the staff and so he's trying to find out more about me than I want to let on, but he's not doing it overtly, he just leaves long spaces that I think he thinks I'll fill. Like I said, clever this one. I tell him a bit about my working background, a bit about the other work that I do, and a bit about what job I would like to have in the future, but that is it – that seems to keep him satisfied and we leave it at that.

Before the end of the month a poster appears on the staff notice board informing us of a mandatory staff meeting which again causes disturbance in the ranks. In all my time here, I don't think that there has been so much attention on the staff and we have certainly never had a staff meeting before. Speculation about the meeting is rife, but none of us are expecting what we are told.

"I have never seen such a shocking lack of professionalism amongst a body of staff" he says. I can practically see people rocking back in their chairs as though they have been punched. He goes on just as calmly – "There is going to have to be a significant change in attitude for many of you, perhaps even most of, and this unit is going to be run for the benefit of the patients. I think some of you have forgotten that you are here for their benefit, and somehow have come to think of the unit being here for the benefit of you to earn a wage. Allow me to be clear on this, you will raise your professional standards, or I will have no hesitation in helping you leave."

There is some ill-advised outrage at this, and one person asks what he means by unprofessional behaviour. In the same measured tone he gives numerous examples of poor conduct – poorly managed break times, staff being made to work in isolation, poor record keeping, inappropriate comments at work about colleagues and patients, this, that – once or twice there's a bit of ill-advised rejection of the list of failings but each time he is ready with examples and has no hesitation in turning the issues straight back on the complainers.

All the time he is calmly surveying the room, not singling anyone out unless they are foolish enough to throw themselves forward, and all the time I am unable to raise my head for the fear of everyone seeing the smile spreading across my face. Like I said, clever man, this one, and he has already got the measure of some of these people. Afterwards no one is happy. One of them, a big fat girl called Bernice, tries to involve me in running him down.

"Who the fuck does he think he is?" she spits.

"Well, I think he thinks he's the manager, and he is" I reply. I am not sure what she thinks of this as about five different expressions try to settle on her face before she just looks back at my face with a confused scowl.

"Well, he can't talk to us like that!" she roars.

"Actually, I really think he can" I say – which I realise is not going to win me any friends today, but I feel the need to point out the stupidity of that last statement. In reply I get a look of contempt before she waddles off to find someone who shares her point of view. Fortunately for her overloaded heart she won't have to walk far.

Later, I am at home I am lying on Christiana's bed with her whilst she is watching some English show that I stopped trying to follow almost as soon as she put it on. She is happy just to lay with me whilst I have my arm around her, and I'm happy just for the time with her. I start thinking about work, though, and about the meeting today. I think about how it is a good thing that someone else has finally seen some of these people for the kind of people they are. I think he is going to be in for a hard time. I also think about Bernice afterwards and how I felt compelled to defend him immediately – I can feel myself frown at this – even though he seems perfectly capable of defending himself, something in me made me leap to his defence.

This is not like me – I have learned that the best way to avoid trouble at work is to avoid ever saying what I think about it, and yet after one comment from a foolish girl I felt my hackles rise.

Interesting.

Dee

I cancel a lot of on call work over the next few weeks, telling my boss that I need the time to prepare for the wedding. Full truth told I don't want to be seeing quite so much of Simon – he made a fool out of me, and I made a fool out of myself over some silly infatuation. I tell myself that the whole thing has just been pre-commitment nerves, something I should have had the maturity to see sooner and deal with.

I can't truthfully say that I forget all about him, but once I stop going out of the way to see him, I do see a lot less of him and think about him a lot less too.

It comes as a shock when I almost literally bump into Simon as I am crossing the hospital car park – it is a few days to the wedding, and I am on my way to meet my mother for the final dress fitting.

I remember it was a bit of a drizzly day and I had my head bowed low out of the rain and was hurrying along so that I practically walked into him before I noticed there was anyone there at all, let alone Simon.

"Hey you! Steady on there, you nearly had me over!"

"Oh! OH! Simon! How are you, I didn't see you there!" – I can feel my cheeks reddening.

"None too bad, thanks – how are you? I haven't seen you in a while!"

I can feel myself smiling at this – I fight the urge to say, "So you missed me then?" and lose.

"Of course!" he exclaims, "It hasn't been the same without you! And I wanted to say goodbye too"

"Wh-wh-what?" I stammer, "What are you talking about? Where are you going? When?" – I don't know if I sound panicked, but I feel like I must do.

"Today – this afternoon in fact. I'm just packing up my stuff and taking it all home"

"Your stuff?"

"Yes, I've been staying at the Hospital when I work – I have one of the flats back there" he nods in the direction of the hospital accommodation block, "and I quit last week, so today I am packing up. I am pleased to see you, I thought I wasn't going to get a chance to properly say goodbye"

This is all news to me: a) that he missed me, b) that he has quit, c) that this could be the last time I see him and d) he was living here, right here, on the hospital grounds.

"Have you got time for a drink?" he says.

I really haven't, and I so want to go. I want to tell him that I have spent so much time thinking about him, that I look forward to just catching sight of him at work, that I long for the occasions when he strides over to me and puts his arms around me, that once, just once, I want him to kiss me.

"I've got to go", I say, "but how about a goodbye kiss?"

He doesn't hesitate – he smiles, puts his arms around me and pulls me tightly to him. We kiss – softly, on the mouth – and pull back slightly to look at each other. Then we kiss again, and again, harder and more passionately. Before I know it, we are standing in a hospital car park in the rain, my umbrella discarded, for want of a better word snogging. I can feel his passion rising for me, his hands holding me in the small of the back, then pulling my hips towards him, his large hands gently squeezing my backside. I have both of my hands in his hair, holding his face to mine. I can feel a heat in me that I have not felt in a long time – if I have ever felt it at all.

We break off kissing, but we are still holding each other – "It's a pity I didn't know you lived here, I might have taken advantage of you", I say.

"You can come over now, if you like?"

I so want to.

"I can't – I really have to go. Will you call me? Maybe we can meet up another time?"

We separate and exchange phone numbers. We say goodbye, then he picks up my umbrella for me. He places one hand on my cheek and kisses me again, tenderly. I have no idea whether he watches me leave because I dare not turn around to look. I walk off to meet Mother and think that

I will never see him again, that whatever chance we had is gone.

Mother is in a state when I see her – I am a few minutes late, and she has spent those few minutes winding herself up into a panic.

"Where on earth have YOU been?" is her opening remark, "LOOK at the state of you!" is her follow up.

"Oh, for God's sake, Mother, it's just a bit of rain" I say.

I spend the next hour being fussed over, pulled about, pinched, poked and on one occasion lightly stabbed with a pin. On balance, this was not a good day.

Ella

Sure enough I eventually return Sepp's call – he seems genuinely pleased to hear from me – and we arrange to meet up in town the following week. I tell him I'll be bringing Anna along and despite a brief pause he rallies well and says he knows a friend who he can bring along and we'll "make a night of it" – I'm a little uncertain as to what he means by that, but when he says it, he doesn't sound the least bit sinister so I let it go.

We agree to meet at the Old Lion but don't say much more than "bye" and "see you next week". When I put the phone down, I turn to Anna who if she had been sitting listening any closer would have been sitting in my lap. She is beaming from ear to ear.

"Ooo a date with a handsome man!" she says.

"You haven't even met him, you don't know what he looks like" I reply.

"Not my date, you fool! I'm taking about you and Sepp!" – she almost sings 'Sepp' as she says it, and I know that she is teasing me, but I can't help my face from flushing and hiding behind my sleeve. She laughs at my obvious discomfort, and pushes me over onto the bed, before standing and crossing the room to my wardrobe.

"Let's have a look at what we've got to work with" she says, opening the door and randomly pulling out clothes which she promptly dumps on the bed, mostly on top of me.

"It's not until next week" I complain from under the pile.

"Yes, but look at what we've got here – greys, blacks, dark green – it's just as well you're not meeting in a forest, or he'd never see you. It won't do, none of it will."

She stands there, arms akimbo, and sighs loudly.

"There's nothing for it, I'm going to have to take you shopping immediately".

I struggle out from the clothes although something has managed to get caught around my head and I can't seem to get it off. I give up and plaintively repeat that it's not until next week.

"Yes, my love, but these things take time – we must plan this so that you are looking perfect!"

She is off out of the room and down the hallway.

"Where are you going? Wait!!" I call to no avail. I untangle myself and hurry off after her. When I catch up with her, she is already downstairs and in the kitchen, heading determinedly towards Sabine.

"We have to take her shopping ", she says, not turning around and indicating me with a thumb over her shoulder.

"But it's not until next week!" I wail.

Sabine looks puzzled, looking back and forth between us. "What's not until next week? Why has she got to go shopping?"

"She's got a date with handsome man and has nothing to go in."

"I never said he was handsome! And I've got plenty of things to go in," I complain "it's just that right now they're all over – "

"Your wardrobe is a disaster in camouflage" says Anna, again over her shoulder without really looking back.

"Right, well let's see what we have to work with" says Sabine, and before long we are all back in my bedroom, only this time there's two of them standing there with arms akimbo, sighing. Sabine casts a critical eye of the assortment of clothes which by now cover most of the available surfaces.

"I have clearly been neglectful in my duties" says Sabine, mock grimly. "This is far more serious than I thought"

"But it's just a date! It might not even *be* a real date! And it's not until next week!" I sound like I am wailing.

"My little Lebski, even your underwear is black or grey and none of it matches – I don't think I can see a primary colour anywhere!"

This is untrue, although I have to admit, not by much.

"Anna, let Olek know we're all going out, I'll go and find my car keys and you…" she trails off and shakes her head a little.

"But why do I need matching underwear? It's not as if he's going to *see* it! And it's not until next week!"

Despite my fairly feeble protests we're soon all in the car, Sabine and Anna up front, and me in the back, still protesting at the urgency of all this. In reply I get a lecture from Sabine about the importance of matching underwear even though "he better NOT" be seeing any of it. It is all about how it will make me feel, apparently. Anna and Sabine seem to be almost oblivious to me otherwise and talk constantly and matter-of-factly about pastels, patterns, something called 'hang' which, evidently, will be very important for someone of my frame along with a definite no heels approach. He is not going to want me towering over him, they say, which I can't help finding mildly hurtful although I know it's not said with any intent. Apparently, it is a source of some mutual dismay that I was previously unaware of that I have underpants "the size of Naples". I am not at all happy to have this discussion and resolve to sit crossly in the back seat with my arms folded.

I realise suddenly that we have not headed north to Dijon but are travelling south. I ask about this and am informed that we off to Lyon where we can expect to find some of the very latest styles – "there's a fashion school there, didn't you know?" – I cannot think for a moment why I would know but don't comment. I settle myself in on the back seat and just watch the countryside go by and listen to the plans Anna and Sabine are making for me.

After a little while I can't help but smile.

The day goes by in a whirlwind of shops, bags, and clothes – Sabine certainly has an eye for bright colours and would travel at the speed of light if she could, but at least Anna is there to provide restraint when needed – she can be very diplomatic with Sabine in a way I have not seen her be with anyone else. It makes me wonder if there is a deeper relationship between these two women that only they know about – nothing romantic, but there are moments when Anna almost seems like the grown-up, and Sabine the petulant teenager, as Anna carefully guides her away from this choice or that course of action, without causing any friction.

I end up having my hair cut as well, because according to Sabine I look like a straw man, but to the newly discovered diplomat in our little band "it's probably been a while since I last had a trim". Sabine has a "tidy-up" at the same time, fussing over the smallest of details in the cut or styling, whilst Anna sits in the back reading fashion magazines. We arrive back home late, and I don't know about the others, but I am certainly footsore and fatigued. There's bread, wine, and cheese for supper, Olek by his own admission being of little use in the kitchen, before an exhausted sleep – I have to rely upon Anna to save me from a mini fashion show straight after supper, because if I look half as tired as I feel I must look ready for the grave – but admittedly with fabulous hair.

A review of the day's purchases is essential the following day, however, although I suspect that the period of grace I am given is more because Olek is out in the vineyards until the afternoon, and without him there is no one to impress. He good-naturedly sits and waits while outfits are changed and arranged (mostly by Sabine) and makes all the right appreciative noises, which makes Sabine happy. Out of the collection I particularly like a simple sky-blue dress with white polka dots and white shoes, and I decide that this is the outfit for when Anna and I go to meet Sepp and his friend.

Once our little fashion parade is over, I try again to give Sabine some money for everything she's bought – all day I would try and press money into the hand of the cashier, or into Sabine's hand, to repeatedly have it politely, yet firmly, pushed away. As Olek is here I hope to have more luck in getting her to take my money, but if anything, it is harder.

"Why?", asks Olek.

"Well, you've paid for all these clothes, and the haircut and-"

"My darling girl, you are our family", says Sabine.

"I know, but I can't expect-"

"Did you? Did you expect?" says Olek, sharply.

"Well, no, but-"

"Well, there we are!" exclaims Olek "we know that you don't expect this from us, but you are our family, and it gives us great pleasure to see you looking so wonderful and it gives me great pleasure to see my wife looking so happy" – Sabine looks at Olek fondly at this point and squeezes his arm. "I may be more outnumbered than I used to be, but since the day you came to us it has been my honour to look after my brother's daughter as though she were my own. Let's hear no more about money, eh? Tell me about this boy."

Unfortunately, I can't give him much – I don't know where he lives, or what he does, or how old he is, or anything really except that he is Polish too. I promise faithfully that if things look like a second date is coming up that I will bring him over to the vineyards so that Olek can "size him up, look him in the eye and shake him by the hand. You can tell a lot about a man by doing that".

For a moment, though, I think about Olek and Sabine – a child could not wish for two more loving parents, and I think about them taking me in, and I think about Anna, and that she is as much a part of the family as I am. I think about the closeness of the four of us, and for a moment I think about the children missing from Olek and Sabine's life, and the love that they have to share with people, not least of which Anna and me. And then, more so than ever before, I feel like I am home.

Dee

I'm not expecting anything unusual when the message tone on my phone goes – it rings a lot – but I am more than a little taken aback when I see who it's from.

> Sorry it's been a while, thought I'd get in touch to see how you've been. Text me back when you can. Simon x

It has been months – literally months – since that rainy day in the car park. When I hadn't heard anything after the first couple of weeks, I assumed I never would, and wrote the whole thing off to experience, to pre-wedding jitters, and promptly removed his number from my contacts. Now – today – I can't remember the last time I thought of Simon, I can't remember the last time I even thought about the car park. I convince myself that this must be another Simon that I know, and even go through my mobile's phonebook to check if the number matches and for some reason this other Simon's name has just not been displayed, but no, no other Simon.

How have I been? Happy, I suppose – the wedding itself I can barely remember, it went by in what seemed like a few seconds before I am on a plane, exhausted, to Barbados. Club Class, of course. I have been on holiday again since, hiking in Scotland - the one thing I would say about Ben is that he shares my love for travel, and now we have a decent joint income there's plenty of opportunity.

How have I been? What does he mean by that, anyway? Was he expecting me to reply and say I have been hanging on the end of the phone waiting for his text message? I engage in an ill-advised period of over examining this simple question repeatedly. Each section of the text message then gets the same treatment – "Sorry it's been a while" is what he said. "A while" hardly describes the months between then and now, 'a while' is a couple of weeks, at most. In hindsight I realise that this is just an excuse to avoid thinking about whether I am going to reply and trying to convince myself that I am going to make a choice here, whereas the truth is that I suspect that I have already decided. The truth is that I am thinking more about what I am going to reply with, rather than whether I am going to.

I think I show incredible restraint by not texting back straight away although in fairness I only manage an hour and that is more likely because I am running samples when his message came in.

> I'm fine thanks – how are you

I debate with myself for a minute or two, typing it in, deleting it, then typing it in again.

> I'm fine thanks – how are you x

Simple, straightforward, to the point – and everyone puts x at the end of their text messages anyway, so it doesn't have to mean anything.

The reply comes almost straight away

> I'm not too bad thanks. Thought I'd get in touch and see how you were, it's been too long hasn't it? I wondered if you'd like to meet up for that drink I owe you? Xx

Two days later I am on a train to Cambridge, going to meet Simon. He is working in some sort of general manager post but gets to travel all over East Anglia visiting various offices of the company he's now working for, in his words "sorting them out". We agree to meet in Cambridge as it is an easy train journey for me and he knows the city well, apparently, from when he used to work there before. I am full of trepidation as the train sets off, and by the time I have boarded the train I have checked with him twice that the meeting is still on. I text to check with him once more from the train to be told that he is already at Cambridge Station, waiting for me.

When I step down onto the platform, I don't see him at first, but as I head toward the exit I see him striding toward me, a beaming smile on his face. He doesn't pause to say hello, or ask how the journey was or anything, he just sweeps me up into his arms and kisses me and kisses me and kisses me, like I am some sort of returned soldier from some distant front. I struggle to catch my breath; I am consumed in his eyes, lost in his hold on me, oblivious to everything and everyone apart from this tall, handsome man who makes me feel like this. I have read about the dizzying effect men are supposed to have on women in everything from magazines to novels, and never believed any of it until this moment. The train has long pulled out from the platform by the time my senses return, the crowd dispersed – no one paid us any attention, standing in the middle of the platform lost in each other. He puts his arm around my waist as starts guiding me to the exit.

"Hungry?" he says, and this is the first words either of us have spoken since I arrived.

"Not really, no" I say – and I'm not, although it is past lunchtime. The combination of butterflies and dizziness have put paid to any hunger pangs I might have had.

"Well, let's find somewhere we can go for that drink, then. I know a couple of decent places –"

"Actually, I'd rather go to somewhere with a bed" – I hear myself say these words, but I can't quite believe that I have.

If he is shocked at all, he doesn't show it. He smiles at me at shows me to his car – we kiss every few steps on the way and again when we're sitting in the front seats.

To be honest I was hoping that he'd take me to his flat, or house or whatever it is that he's got, but I soon learn that he lives in Kings Lynn, which is miles away, and both he and I have only the afternoon together – I have to get back for a night out with Sarah that we've had booked for weeks, he has to report back to his main office before the end of the day, so I am a little disappointed when we pull into a hotel car park outside the city. He takes care of everything, though, booking us a room and dealing with the receptionists. I can't help thinking that they're looking at us knowing exactly what we're up to, but I really don't care. We go to our room and he and I pour out our desires onto one another – there is very little talking, our bodies and our hands saying everything that needs to be said, and loudly. We are not even as far into the room as the bed by the time my blouse is gone and his suit jacket and shirt gone the same way. There is almost a desperation to the way he is kissing me, a desire for me that I have never felt from anyone, anytime ever – his mouth is on mine, on my neck, on my shoulders, on my chest, exploring every square inch of skin. Then his hands undo my bra and I can feel the ache in my breasts and nipples to have the same attention from his hungry mouth, and it is not long before they are rewarded – I gasp as he takes each nipple in turn into his mouth and luxuriates on them with his tongue. I can feel that I am panting with excitement, with the ferocity of his need to explore me. I pull at my skirt and panties before pulling at his belt buckle and trousers, and in doing so I feel what I have wanted from him in so long, I feel his desire for me pressed against my hands. With his trousers opened I reach into boxers and hold and caress his manhood, whilst he guides me to the bed – I willingly fall onto it, kicking away my skirt and panties, whilst he finishes his undressing.

I want him to plunge straight into me, reward my wait for him by making me wait no longer, but he has not finished exploring my body yet – his tongue traces lines across my body, his fingers seek out my mound and dive into me. I gasp, I almost shout out, I am pulling him toward me, kissing him whenever he is close enough for me to reach. I have never felt as alive as this, as turned on as this, as so damn wet as this, and I deserve to have him inside me. He finally looks up from between my thighs, smiles at me and then brings himself up my body, kissing my skin on the way. I feel him push into me – there's no fumbling, no need to guide him there – and I feel like I could faint. I yell out, I grab onto his back so hard that I later see blood there where my nails have dug in, and I urge him into moving harder and faster and deeper inside of me. There is no holding back either of us, I feel bruised almost, but it is such a good feeling I urge him on more, locking our mouths together, my hands in his hair again, his gripping my breasts, my thighs or my ass.

When we climax it is together, and it is unlike anything I have ever experienced – nothing I have done with another man or on my own has even approached this, I am adrift in an orgasm that seems to go on for ages, pulse after pulse of intense sensations flowing through me. I am spent. I am ecstatic.

Simon is not done with me yet, though.

Almost immediately he is exploring my body again, his tongue seeking out my pussy and diving into it, sweeping over my clit. I am shaking, I cannot help but cry out and moan at the things he is doing to me, the orgasm I thought would never end crashes back into me again and I do shout out, and grab at his head to force it harder between my legs. He makes me cum again and again, with his mouth, with his fingers, with his cock; he has me on my back, on my knees on the bed whilst he drives into me from behind so hard that I am gripping onto the sheets until my knuckles turn white. I want this never to end; I never want to be without this man making me feel the way he is making me feel now. I didn't know that I could be made to feel like this, let alone that I could be made to feel like this over and over and over and over. He plays my body like it is an instrument, he seems to know instinctively where to touch, where to kiss, when to be tender and when to be hard. I love it, I love it all so much.

We sleep after a couple of hours, neither of us climb under the duvet, he just lays back, draws me to him and I lay my head on his chest, and eventually our breathing returns to normal, and then to the slow, deep pace of sleep. I don't think a single word has been exchanged since we came into this room, and here we are asleep in each other's arms. I am awoken by gentle kisses and tender caresses, and we make love again with more tenderness and less intensity for exactly the same outcome. We shower together and he washes every inch of me, gently kissing my body as he does so – we say very little if anything at all, perhaps both imagining that words spoken will break the spell, but after our shower we discuss the practicalities of getting me back to the station to catch the train home.

I feel more ill-at-ease as we leave the hotel, more aware that it must be entirely obvious to the receptionists exactly why we came here today, and I am probably brooding over this for the car journey to the station, meaning that there is very little in the way of conversation then either. We arrive in time for us to share another minutes' kissing before my train pulls in – Simon comes with me the train side, holding hands with me as we walk. We say goodbye with a promise to see each other soon, and I don't know in my heart whether I dare to believe in it.

I don't let him see but as the train pulls away there are tears in my eyes.

Ella

I am packing again, but this time I don't have to do it all in secret, although in some ways I think I would have preferred that.

Sepp and I have been together for almost two years, Diane is going to school soon and both he and I are going to need to find work.

Sepp has been a builder for all his working life, but for the last few months hasn't been able to get anything more than a couple of days labouring at a time. Olek has offered him work at the vineyard which he turned down for reasons of his own – perhaps he didn't want to be beholden to his girlfriend's uncle, I don't know his reasoning, but after many evenings with his friends in the taverns about Dijon he's decided that his (and, therefore, our) best prospects lie in moving to Britain – he's heard that there is plenty of work there for willing men and that he can get paid a good rate as a builder. I am anxious about the possibility of going, but Sepp has it all planned out – he will get a job, we'll get a flat and I'll take care of it, and him. Since being out of work there has been a bitterness to him which I hadn't seen before so I promise myself that I'll do all I can to make things better for him, and if that means moving to another country again, then so be it.

Unlike her usual self, Sabine says little about our proposed move. She doesn't discuss with me, doesn't comment about it when I mention it, doesn't react to any bit of information or news that I have to impart about it. She listens and smiles politely at the plans I have outlined for her, but as for what she thinks about it I have no idea.

"Is it what you want to do?" she asked me once. I said that it would be another experience to have and that I had to do what I could to help Sepp.

"But is it what *you* want to do?" she asked again. I must have looked confused because when I didn't answer she just enveloped me in her shawl as she hugged me and kissed me on the head.

And that has been the most I can get out of her on the subject.

Anna, on the other hand, has been enthusiastic to the point of bursting. She has been planning to come to visit me once we are settled in, and together we have been brushing up on our English. In the privacy of her quarters, she has revealed to me that she is looking to move on from Olek's vineyard and find her own way in the world, and I can tell that this talk of living in a different country has really caught her attention – to hear her talk about it you would think that it is her moving, not me. I hope that she does keep good on her promise of coming to see me, it will be hard enough leaving Olek and Sabine and the family that we have become in the last few years without imagining the prospect of never again sitting up late at night and sharing a bottle of wine with Anna.

There is probably at least as much planning goes into a move that everyone knows about as there is for the secret trip I took a few years ago. Packing and sorting makes me think back to that time and the reasons why I left there – there I wasn't wanted, here I am, so why leave? But Sepp is adamant that we will be better off so that's that. I told him that I have no idea what kind of work I can get, an unqualified woman in her twenties unless there was a large call for French-Polish translators in England that no one had mentioned, but it isn't something that we have discussed in any length, he's certain that "something will come up".

The bitterness that has come over Sepp has made it difficult to talk to him about things properly – when we first got together, he wanted to know about me and spent time and money making me feel special. That first date we ate and drank and danced, and he insisted on paying for everything (Anna's date, incidentally, turned out to be "a shaved ape with manners and hygiene to match", according to her – I don't think that they ever saw one another again). He was the perfect gentleman – kind and polite and making sure I was home by midnight to find Olek and Sabine on the doorstep – he shook Olek's hand that night and told him that he had a lovely daughter, to which he replied "actually, I have two" as Anna disappeared inside. We didn't even kiss until the third date, just a kiss on the cheek from him before I went inside – it took until about the sixth or seventh date before Olek stopped meeting me on the doorstep, and probably until the tenth or twelfth until Sabine stopped.

Sepp must have known that I was inexperienced in affairs of the heart, and he never openly pressed me for more than I was willing to give, but somehow, I always felt that I was letting him down in some way. The first time we had sex I convinced him that I really wanted to, and that I had enjoyed it, but neither was true – I had convinced myself that he was slipping away from me, because he was becoming more distant and thought that that would let him know how seriously I thought about our relationship. Then once we had done it once he seemed to think that it was expected and I didn't want to let him know that I really wasn't that bothered about it at best, and at worst positively hated it. Once or twice, he would complain about leading him on before turning his approaches down, but if I had been leading him on then that was certainly news to me.

Apart from that, though, he still would want to treat me to a meal out or to some flowers or a new book or a trip to the cinema. I couldn't complain about that. Having no job, though, made it more difficult for him to treat me and instead he wanted to stay in at the flat he shared with an old friend of his so that they could play Xbox for hours whilst I sat at the end of the sofa, or washed up a week's worth of dishes that they had left, or simply fell asleep, so when he started talking about the opportunities he'd have in the UK, and started making plans for us both, I could see the logic behind it and thought how that would make things easier for him to be the man I had first met.

Hence the packing – I have far more stuff than I came with, not least of which clothes which I am going to have to pare down significantly and decide upon what I most will need. A lot of trousers (it is cold in England), jumpers, long sleeved tee-shirts…I pick up my blue and white polka dot dress and put it in my 'to pack' pile, but many of my dresses will stay here. I am not going to take as many books this time, partly because I learned the lesson about the weight of books the hard way the last time I moved, and partly because I don't think I'll have many places to put them when I get there – we're due to stay with one of Sepp's builder friends who is working in the UK already whilst he finds work and we find a place to live.

In the end Olek gives me a large wedge of notes and tells me to put it somewhere safe, somewhere only I know about, and not to tell anyone about it.

"For emergencies" he says, "a deposit on a flat if you need it or a plane ticket back home if it doesn't work out, whatever". I hug him and I hold him for the longest time, I thank him and give him a kiss on the cheek, trying extremely hard not to cry at the simple kindness of this lovely man. He just nods quietly once and walks out of my room leaving me to my packing.

This is not the only surprise – within two hours of the time I am due to be picked up by Sepp to head for the airport, Anna announces that she is coming with us – she has packed, has paid for her own ticket and has enough money to start renting a flat as soon as we get there. I can't help casting an eye toward Olek at this point, but he remains almost expressionless. Sabine has been remarkably absent for the few hours leading up to what was my and is now our departure, and last night's supper was a very stilted affair, not the usual dinner table conversation. As I think on this, I start to have an inkling into the importance that Anna and I have had in Sabine and Olek's lives, and I become certain that there was some degree of suggestion in Anna coming with me, and that Anna was also in receipt of a donation from Olek that must not be mentioned. It is almost time for me to be picked up when Sabine appears, looking at her most beautiful and immaculate as I have ever seen her. I can see that she is working hard at not letting go of her emotions though, and I can also see that this is likely to be a battle she is going to lose. She hugs Anna, kisses her on the forehead and tells her she will always be welcome here, and to take care of her sister. When she turns to me, I can see the defences are nearly almost gone and when she hugs me I can feel the sobs wracking her body. She holds me for long enough to compose herself, then taking hold of my hands she tells me that this is my home, that this is my family, and that no matter where I am I will always be in their hearts. She says this through broken sobs and deep breaths as she tries to get her message out and finishes by telling me to take care of my sister. I can see Anna wiping away tears and Olek looking away as though temporarily distracted, although I know there is a tear in his eye too.

As the taxi pulls up with Sepp on board the four of us are embracing on the yard. It is a beautiful day at the vineyard, and I know that I am going to remember this moment, this feeling, for as long as I live, encapsulated in the love of these three people.

Dee

This is how it goes for the next few months – one or other of us will book a hotel for the night and meet up. We meet in London, Leeds, Reading, in everything from budget roadside hotels to high-end country house type places. Without discussing it we have taken turns in paying for the bookings and we meet early and leave late. I never have a problem getting away from home, I have always been inclined to spending one or two nights a week out with friends or visiting people and Ben has gotten used to me staying out all night, often with short notice. I am quite sure nothing appears untoward when I'm meeting Simon.

However, I cannot say the same about work – we text each other a lot, always when I am at work, and it always gets very steamy – and it's been noticed that I am smiling a lot more and that it is always around the time I get text messages. I know this because Rebecca, one of the junior technicians, sidled up to me one lunch time, and comes straight out with it.

"Have you got a fancy man?" she says. I try to look a little shocked at the suggestion, but I must just look as guilty as anything because I don't need to answer.

"Oooh so you have! I've noticed you spending a lot more time looking at your phone and that you always seem happier afterwards. That and you used to keep your phone in your locker and now it's always in your pocket". This is true, we shouldn't really have phones in the lab and up until recently I would have been a stickler for this. No one else seemed to bother or worry about it so I didn't think anyone would notice. I can see now, though, that this is a big change that I should have been aware of.

"It's nothing, it's just a friend" I say, lamely.

"Oh, it's alright, I'm not about to dob you in or anything – if you want a bit on the side and it makes you happier, why not?". This is the first that I have thought that anyone else could have thought that I was unhappy in the first place – I don't know if it's being married or being married to Ben that is the problem, but I think that it's Ben. He is just so…so… so just Ben, I suppose. He doesn't excite me or make me feel pleased to see him, he's just…there.

"Oh, it's nothing," I say, "we just flirt a bit, that's all. We've always got on well and he knows I'm married, and he's married so…"

This is another reason why the text messages always take place in work time – he has since told me that he's married, although I have to say that it didn't bother me at all. At the times when we are together, he is all mine, and I am all his and that is all that counts.

At first, I want to try and leave this conversation alone, but Rebecca wants to know all about him, and I start to feel like I want to tell her about him, to tell anyone about him. I don't tell her during that lunch break, but I do tell her a couple of days later that we see each other as often as we can and a little about how he makes me feel. "Good for you!" is her response to that, and she hugs me warmly which takes me aback a little.

I don't know why I shared all of this with Rebecca, a younger woman and a subordinate that I barely know, and for a while I worry that she'll spread it around the lab, but the most I have a probably a few warmer smiles from her and the opportunity to have someone to talk to about it.

I discuss it with her when I notice a change in Simon's behaviour. We are walking from the lab to one of the more distant wards with four packs of O negative.

"He wanted to go for a walk" I tell her.

"So? So, what's wrong with that?"

"We've never been for a walk. He wanted to go for a walk with me and he wanted to hold hands as we went."

"So did you?"

"Well...yes. What else could I do?"

"And?"

"And what?"

"And what was it like?"

I think for a minute back to that evening – we had been sitting in the restaurant at the hotel just after dinner (we had already been in the room for about four hours before then) and whereas usually we'd just head back to the room he wanted to go out for a walk with me. I couldn't understand why at all, but I went along with it anyway although I couldn't help thinking that I'd rather have gone back to the room. We had walked a short distance when he just reached down and held my hand as we walked.

"It was different – he holds hands differently"

"Huh? How can you hold hands differently?"

I show her what I mean by holding hands with her in the corridor.

"He holds hands like *this*..." I interlock our fingers and we walk for a bit "whereas I'd normally hold hands like *this*" I hold her hand by crossing our palm so that our fingers hook over the edge of each other's hand. We walk along like that for a bit to get the feel of it.

We swap the two positions a few times as we're walking along, before she bursts out laughing.

"What's so funny?"

"It's just that we have spent about the last five minutes walking down the main corridor of the hospital holding hands. You should have seen some of looks we've been getting!"

I flush with embarrassment at this and try to take my hand away.

"No, it's too late to bail out now; everyone will think we're having a tiff. Come on, we've got to see it through to the end now"

She says this with a playful smile, and I think to hell with it and walk all the rest of the way, hand in hand, chatting and occasionally giggling.

"He likes you" she says.

"Well, I'd hope that he does!" I reply

"No, he REALLY likes you. He's beginning to really, REALLY like you."

"You think so?"

"Don't you?"

I haven't thought about it. When I think of Simon I think about the way he makes me feel when we're together, not about movie dates and picking out furniture.

"He's falling for you and at least for a few minutes he wants to feel like you're a proper couple."

By this time, we're nearly at the doors to the ward, and we're still holding hands.

"C'mon lover," she says with a wink, "let's get this done". She pulls me to her, kisses me on the lips quickly, and then is off through the doors leaving me a bit stunned by everything standing in the corridor.

Alina

I am unnerved by this man – he seems to have some sort of x-ray vision that doesn't just see through doors (he has a habit of walking in on carers right when they are in the middle of doing something wrong) but right through people too. He does not accept people not doing their jobs and already there have been people caught out. I have not had to go in front of him, but from what I hear he has some sort of skill for weeding out lies and liars and then dealing with them very harshly.

Naturally, there is barely a good word being said about him by anyone, least of all the fat lazy maintenance man, who seems to have made it his business to undermine Mr Holcroft whenever he can, and consequently do even less work, if that were possible. Work has become quite a hostile place now, and I am seriously thinking of moving on – none of these people are my friends but I can do without hostility at home and at work as well.

Mr Holcroft seems to be totally unaffected by any of this, though – he still smiles serenely at people, be they staff or visitors or patients, he talks to patients, and I haven't heard him so much as raise his voice, although I hear that he is not averse to that once he has you in his office – if the ward gossips are to be believed.

He seems friendly enough with me, although I am always careful to watch what I am saying in front of him because he is the same with everyone, I certainly don't think that he's picking me out for any special treatment. He asks sensible, relevant questions about the work I am doing, about the patients, about the plans for care over the next few days, and every day before he goes home, he'll search out the nurse on duty and make sure that everything is going alright before he leaves.

He is not here doing dressings and bed baths, but it's not unusual for him to still be here at seven or eight in the evening, working on something in his office or going through papers in the nurses' office, or talking things over with patients and visitors. A lot of the care staff say he thinks himself too good to get his hands dirty. I think that he has enough to do without doing their jobs for them as well.

As if to put that to the test, though, after a few days of witnessing whispering in corners and hurriedly stopped conversations when I walk into the break room, about two thirds of the staff due on duty call in sick within a few minutes of each other – I find this out when I come on duty myself expecting handover to me and a few colleagues to find that me, another eastern European care worker and a very young health care assistant are the only ones in. Agnes, a pleasant but older and often forgetful nurse that does night duty, exclaims how the phone has been "ringing off the hook!" since 7.15 am. Between the three of us there is no way that we are going to get through a day of ward patients.

Handover is brief, partially because the extended unrelated chit chat doesn't happen this morning, but mostly because me, Grace and Louise will have to get going early if we are to get things done.

"Call Mr Holcroft" says Agnes as she leaves, "he needs to help you sort this out." Her tone is friendly, and I think she is just giving me a little advice rather than anything more sinister. As the ward door closes behind her, I reflect for a moment and realise that she is right. I dash into the office, find his number and call. Once I have relayed the message about how short staffed we are today he tells me he will be there shortly and I hang up and run back to Grace and Louise to get as much done as we can.

He arrives ten minutes later in a dark blue nursing tunic. I am just struggling to get the medicines trolley out of the store cupboard – it is a large, wheeled thing, all metal and hard corners, and steers like a barge – when he briskly walks up to me and asks where he can start.

"What do you mean?" I say, "you're the boss, you tell me."

"No, Alina, this is your shift, you know the routine far better than I do, you tell me where to go and what to do" he says, and this is how I imagine his no-nonsense discussions with some of the staff must sound like. There is no prospect of disagreeing with him, so I ask him to take the medicines trolley and I will go and help the other staff. He nods, takes the keys and the medicine charts from me, and steers away the medicine trolley to the end of the ward. I scurry off to get started on patient care.

I don't know when he had done it, but it is clear twenty minutes later that he has made arrangements for extra staff to come from other wards to help us, as three other care assistants come in and each, after a brief word with Mr Holcroft at the trolley is directed toward me. I feel like an army captain, marshalling my troops for battle, directing them here or there to my patients, adapting to their changing needs. I actually find myself enjoying the day – not a moment to stop and think but reacting, relying on my knowledge and skill. I don't see it coming but suddenly all five of my comrades-not-in-arms are in front of me asking what needs to be done next, and I realise that we have finished our morning duties, and much earlier than is usual.

I go to where I see Mr Holcroft talking to an elderly male patient whilst he measures out the man's medications – they seem to be having a conversation, although I know for a fact that the patient has profound dementia and meaningful conversation is, at least for the moment, beyond him.

"We are done" I announce, "I will take over from here".

"No thanks, Alina – can you organise some breaks for the ladies and make sure you all get a sit down and a cup of tea please" he replies. I speak to the staff and get it organised then head back to where he is now, in between patients, and put my hand on the handle of the medicines trolley.

Gently but firmly, he steers the trolley away from me.

"You too" he says, with a look that does not invite discussion.

I scurry off again.

The afternoon shift arrives without incident, and for the first time that I can remember I feel like I have had a good day at work. This lasts until I get home. Most days I am home just after Christiana – unless she has an after-school club – but Mama is there to take care of her until I get home. Today I barely have my key in the door before Mama is there – she has been crying, I can see, and looks very distressed.

All she can do is repeat "Imi pare rau" over and over again. She has never learned English.

"Mama, what is it?" I ask urgently – Mama says nothing I can make out and is wringing her hands and crying again. I take her gently by the shoulders and look into her face.

"Mama, what is it?" I ask more gently. Her face is crumpled, and she is sobbing quietly. Then I realise that the flat is unnaturally quiet – normally I would come in to the TV on Christiana spread out on the settee. I go to push past Mama but she grabs on to my arm and tries to pull me back, "I'm sorry, no darling, don't look, I'm sorry".

My blood chills – I can feel my expression harden and I snatch my arm away from her.

"What have you done?" I spit. I am so angry I feel the colour drain from my face as I stare into hers. I turn sharply leaving Mama by the door as I march down the hallway.

"Christiana?" I call as I approach the lounge – but when I open the door she is not there – except for not having a teenager sprawled on the couch and no cartoons on the TV everything looks normal. As I turn back toward her bedroom, I glare at Mama who hasn't moved except to support herself against the door frame and I feel a sense of puzzlement.

As I gently knock on the door and turn the handle of her bedroom door I call out for Christiana again, more quietly than before. She is there, laying on her bed. With another glance back to Mama I walk in and close the door behind me.

"Darling, are you sleeping?" I ask, "Hard day at school?"

She shakes her head but doesn't say anything.

"Everything ok?" I say as I cross the room and sit next to her. I start stroking her hair. Is she sick?

We stay like that for a moment before she turns to me and bursts into tears burying her head in my lap.

The side of her face that has been turned to the wall – her lips, her cheek and her eye – are swollen and deeply purple with an angry bruise.

I draw in a sharp breath – because I don't need to ask her or Mama what has happened any more, I know what has happened – it has happened to me enough that I recognise the signs of a slight girl after a punch in the face.

Ella

England is beautiful, no more so than the vineyards back home, but in a quite different way. The people, for the most part, are pleasant enough, and I quickly find work as care worker in the local hospital – my English is good enough to communicate well with the patients and the staff, and it is a good job. I like being able to talk to the patients – especially the old men – and they smile at me and tell me how good I am and how they look forward to seeing me every day.

It is funny, most people are lovely to me, even though I have an obvious accent and I see in the news on the TV and in the newspapers about the Eastern Europeans coming to Britain. Everybody at work is lovely to me, but Sepp swears about our neighbour who he says makes comments every time he sees Sepp come in or out or go in the garden. He swears about a lot of things these days.

Sepp hasn't been able to get work for the last six months – sure enough, when we got here, he quickly found work as a plasterer on a building site – a huge new hospital on the edge of town that looks all steel and glass and not at all like the hospital I work in. Then one day I found him at home when I got in from work, quiet and angry.

"They got rid of us" he said.

"What? What do you mean they got rid of us?"

"All of us, all of the Poles on the site. Me, Kacper, Szymon...all of us. The foreman marched us all off site, we barely had the time to grab our things"

I notice that Sepp's tool bag is at his feet – normally his tools, if they come in the house at all, are left at the door. He knows what I think about his dirty tools in my clean house, but he is clearly upset, and I don't say anything.

"Just rounded us all up like animals and told us to get off, we weren't welcome!"

"Surely they can't do that?" I say.

"Well, they have" he answers, and kicks his tool bag in frustration. He looks at me as he does so with a guilty flash in his eyes and I can see my education of where his tool bag belongs has not been lost on him, but this is not the time to have that conversation.

I sat beside him and held his hand whilst he told the story.

It turned out that there had been an argument on the site between one of the British men and one of the Polish men which had escalated into a fist fight. The Polish guys thought their man was being attacked so raced to help, while the British men saw a group of Poles rushing toward one of theirs. Neither Sepp, nor Kacper nor Szymon had been involved in the fight, but the next day the foreman had come on to the site and announced that there was going to be less work available as the build moved on and so some men would be leaving the site. According to Sepp the foreman and a couple of other men then went round the site and told anyone that was Polish – or even thought to be Polish when in fact they were Slovak or Czech or Romanian – that there was no more work for them, and they were to leave immediately.

Like I say, that was six months ago. We have survived on what I earn and what Sepp had managed to save whilst he was working, although that is all gone, as is everything Olek gave me. Kacper found work again after a couple of weeks, although Szymon went back to Poland almost immediately – we saw him briefly before he left, bitter and angry.

I know Sepp wants to go too – back to France maybe or perhaps back to Poland, I am not sure – but what I am sure about is that he doesn't feel welcome here and is convinced that he has been blacklisted for construction work now. This was a new concept to me, that building firms will share details about the employees they don't want to have working for them and so it becomes difficult to find work again. I can't see why Sepp might have been on this list and he swears that he can't either, except through some mistaken identity during the fight that started it all.

I don't want to leave though. Sepp's tendency to become morose is back, and I know that I gave him and us the chance to make everything better by coming to England and getting jobs and living and being happy, and by that logic I should want to follow him back again – but I don't. I like my life here; I like the people I work with and the people I look after. I like the countryside and I like the old buildings. I like that for the most part people keep themselves to themselves. I like English pubs (although I especially like the ones that serve Polish beer), and I like the friends I have made at work and the people that I know in the town like the shopkeeper on the corner, and the lady that works in the laundrette and I even like our neighbour. They are kind people who always greet me with a smile, and maybe take the time to have a chat about the weather.

I think again about how different it is here compared to home, then realise that I do think of the vineyard and Olek and Sabine as home, not the orchards of Wroclaw – which makes me think about Anna and it gives me an idea.

Anna lives just the other side of town in a little apartment by herself and we see each other usually about twice a week, usually here or at the pub rather than her tiny place. She is working as a temporary office worker for a company that exports parts or something, so having someone that speaks fluent French has been a real help, or at least so she says. She likes her boss and, according to her, her boss likes her too and she is getting on well. She talks less and less about going back to school than she did, and I can tell that she is enjoying life here too.

I bring up my idea the next time we meet up. We are in the King's Head on the High Street as it is roughly equal distance for us to come to, and by the time we are through the door the bartender who knows us both by now has two opened Tyskies on the bar waiting. Anna goes to pay – she knows how tight money is for me – but I insist, and we take our beers and sit down.

"What is it then?" says Anna as soon as we are seated. "Are you pregnant?"

"What?" I splutter into my bottle, and I feel myself blush and I have to wipe the beer off my chin.

"Are you pregnant? It's just you've been vibrating like a violin string since I saw you *and* insisted that you buy the first beer, so you obviously have something you want to tell me."

"No, I am not pregnant" I say, manage to regain some composure, look at her and shake my head.

"Well it's something big, come on, what is it?"

I say nothing for a moment and pick at the label on the bottle, then at my nail.

"Do you want to move in with me?" I blurt out, so quickly that I think she can't have heard me properly, because she looks at me quizzically for a moment before replying.

"This is all a bit sudden, what's happened to Sepp?"

"Nothing, it's just that we have a spare room, you have that awful flat and…"

"It's not awful!"

"Anna, it's terrible. I hate it and so do you"

Her indignation subsides a little. "It's not that terrible" she sighs, "and I happen to like it. But what does Sepp think about this?". As far as Anna is concerned, Sepp and I live in idyllic pre-marital bliss, albeit with not much money. I haven't told her about how miserable he is all the time, how he has stopped asking to have sex with me because he knows I have no interest in it – in fact, how we rarely go to bed together at the same time or get up at the same time any more, how he has been talking about going home, and in general how I wish that, as much as I love him, I was living with someone who was a bit happier.

"He's fine with it." I lie because he hasn't got a clue that I am doing this. She looks thoughtful for a moment before she tells me that she'll think about it and we move on to talking about everything and nothing, about how her work is going and mine, about some TV show she has seen but I haven't and we relax and laugh and go home at the end of the night after a warm hug.

She calls me the next day.

"Yes" she says, as soon as I answer. It's just after 8am, I am not working today and I am half asleep still having planned a bit of a lie in.

"Yes what?"

"Yes, I'll move in with you. I'll have my things packed by the weekend and be there on Saturday."

Anna has never been one to wait before acting on any decision she has made. Me, on the other hand, well for me it is Tuesday, but I don't tell Sepp that I have asked Anna to come and live with us until Friday night. He takes it well and just moans a little that he will have to be up early on Saturday to clear the spare room out a bit. I tell him I'll help and that seems to be the right thing to say. Anna arrives in her old and rusty little orange car (it looks like it might have been red once) a little after lunchtime, and I am disappointed to see that she has so little stuff with her, mostly just clothes and a few personal items. I mention to her that she hasn't brought any furniture and she tells me she didn't ever get any because her place was furnished and, anyway, there wouldn't have been the space. I can see her point, and perhaps it's just that for someone that seems to fill the room with her personality, they don't need to have all the stuff to fill a room with too.

She insists on paying half the rent even though there are three of us ("I have half the bedrooms") and that's that. Once she is moved in – which doesn't take long – she buys all of us a takeaway and a bottle of wine for her and me. Sepp takes himself off to bed once Anna and I start giggling after about half a bottle. Once we are full of Chinese food and the bottle is empty, we take ourselves off too, but not before Anna throws her arms around me, kisses me and says "Thank you. I bloody hated that flat" and we giggle again.

Alina

It takes much of the next hour, and between the sobs of three distressed women, to establish the exact circumstances of what has happened.

Andrei came home early, much earlier than would usually be expected, reeking of drink and clearly angry about something. He barely, if ever, speaks to or acknowledges Mama anyway so she did her usual thing of staying out of his way and in her room listening out for the door which would indicate Christiana was home. She heard him clatter about in the kitchen then put something in the microwave, then the TV on, loud.

Christiana swears to me that all she did was come home and ask to watch her programme on TV. He told her that she could go and watch it on her portable in her bedroom and she got as far as opening her mouth to say that her TV hasn't worked properly in ages when he leapt up from his armchair, spilling his plate and cutlery on the floor, and told her to keep her fucking mouth shut, before punching her in the face. Mama heard the shouting, the scream and the crash as Christiana fell to the floor and rushed in to see Andrei standing over her, red with rage and fist clenched. He turned as she came in, scowled, then pushed past her grabbing his leather jacket as he went, slamming the front door after him. Once he was gone Christiana ran to her room and refused to come out, leaving Mama to clear up the broken plate.

I feel guilty for the anger I directed at her, and she accepts my apology grudgingly, but only because she does not think I need to apologise. She blames herself for letting Christiana come to harm, despite she and I telling her that she could not have known what would happen and that none of it is her fault. I am just grateful that she was there to walk into the room when she did and am certain that the only reason Andrei did not take his violence any further is because he didn't want a witness.

I don't bother trying to call or text him – I know all too well not to 'annoy' him when he is not at home. With the application of some ice and some anti-inflammatories we manage to bring the swelling and bruising down on her face, and I don't think that there is anything broken. She is lucky that the skin hasn't broken either. I reassure her that she won't be going to school until after it has settled down and we will tell the school and her friends that she has 'flu. As much as can be expected she seems happy with that plan.

The next day I am due in work again – Mama is scared to be left alone with Christiana, but I am sure that there won't be a problem. Andrei didn't come home last night, and I know that when he does, he will be contrite and will probably try to buy Christiana a new TV. Nonetheless I call or text Mama every hour or so just to check that they are alright. Mama assures me that, yes, they are fine, and no, they have not seen Andrei, and yes, she will let me know if he comes home. I have not heard from him either, not that I expected to.

Of course, I have not told anyone at work about any of this. I ignore and am ignored by almost all the staff except for Louise who cannot do enough for me today and smiles at me like I am an angel or something. It is clear from some of the looks I am getting that there is disappointment that the shift yesterday went as well as it did, and the ringmaster, the maintenance man whose usual post is at the reception desk, is much more mobile today as he circulates around to little groups of two and three, obviously consoling them all. Ha!

I see Mr Holcroft from time to time and have been carrying out my duties in my usual manner, so I am surprised when, toward the end of the shift, he asks me to come to the office.

"Sit down" he says, I do. He sits on the edge of his desk, instead of the chair, on my side with his hands crossed in his lap. I am cataloguing everything I did yesterday looking for the fault for the dressing down I am now expecting.

"What's wrong?" he asks.

"Nothing" I reply, "What did you want to see me for?"

"Well, if I were to look at your face south of your nose, I would agree that there is nothing wrong – but the top half is a different story altogether. So – what's wrong?"

I can feel a look of shock and surprise forming, but I quickly pull it back in and compose myself again, although I now I .

feel like I want to cry.

"Nothing at all" I say and smile widely but weakly, "I don't know what you see but I am fine".

"Look, you had a hard day here yesterday, and I want you to know how grateful I am" He looks up at me again, looking thoughtful, almost as if he is scrying a map or an ancient parchment, his gaze switching between my eyes "...but that's not it, is it?". He leaves the question hanging unanswered – but what is it about this man that sees through everything, even through me, and no one sees through me!

"I can't tell you to talk to me, and even if I could I wouldn't want to obligate you, but I want you to know that if there is anything I can to do, if you need someone to talk to, you can talk to me. I don't suppose there are many people here you can confide in, do you have someone out of work?" I just look at him a little nonplussed and shake my head. "Well, look, I am here and am happy to talk to you if you need someone to unload on. You don't have to, but I want you to know that I am here." I nod, because I dare not open my mouth in case it all pours out here, all over the desk and the carpet and the chairs. I feel like there is a crack in the dam, and unless I reinforce it, we will both drown.

After a moment I get up to leave and cross the room. I don't look back but as I walk through the door I pause, still with my back to him, and say, "Thank you" and return to the shift.

Andrei turns up again two days later. I know he is home because there is a brand-new boxed TV against the wall outside Christiana's bedroom. It turns out that Andrei had lost some money over a deal he was making, which is why he has been absent, trying to get the deal back together. What I think he means is that he lost money gambling and has spent the last two days getting drunk and trying to win it back again. The TV stays there, untouched, unmoved, until an argument over a week later when it is snatched up and hurled out of an open window onto the street below to reflect the lack of gratitude that Andrei clearly expects from his wife and daughter. It is gone by morning, as is Andrei again. This time he comes back with new clothes for me, which turn out to be made of large steel rings held together with a black see-through mesh. Just like the TV, this gift is directly related to the argument that caused him to walk out and caused the TV to take flying lessons.

I don't end up with a black eye the day he comes home again, and later I hate myself because I don't.

Dee

It is some months later before I see Simon again – this time he is at a nursing conference and is in London for it. I know he has moved on a couple of jobs and a couple of new towns but although we haven't seen much of each other we have stayed in touch.

I know he is single again although not yet divorced – he told me – and although I neither want nor to discuss being in a proper relationship with him, I think about what that might be like. I do daydream about him, especially when we text, and even more so if we have been a bit steamy in our messages.

We are laying naked in bed together when I ask him about why he is getting divorced.

"I didn't love her" he says, matter of factly. For a moment I think about how unfair that is of him to have married someone that he didn't love, but then I remember my own circumstances and how unfair I am being to Ben, and say nothing.

"I knew I didn't love her before the wedding" he continues "and I even tried to get out of it. I kind of got engaged to her by accident when we were drunk one night, and it spiralled from there, and I knew that I had to try and stop it. But by then there was so much pressure from everyone to see it through and I just put it all down to cold feet. So, I did, I went through with it and for a while it was OK – it wasn't spectacular, but it wasn't terrible either. Then I started noticing things that I had either ignored or didn't notice before, like she is very mean to people – especially her Mum – and is never at fault for anything."

He stops talking, not, I sense, through any discomfort, just because there isn't any more to say on the subject as far as he is concerned.

"Have you ever been in love?" I ask.

"Of course!"

We lapse back into silence.

I am almost asleep on his chest when he says, "You do know I love you, right?"

"What?"

"You do know I love you, Dee? I wouldn't be able to be a part of this, nor do the things that we do together, if I didn't love you."

Naturally, I feel a thrill when I hear this – and my mind briefly flicks through some of the things we do together, indeed some of the things we have done this afternoon. My pussy feels both sore from the afternoon's activities and stirred into wakefulness by this train of thought. I set this aside, though, and ask the first thing that comes into my head.

"Do you think you will fall in love with me?" Where did that come from?

"Dee, I do love you, but I am well aware of your situation, and I know you don't want to talk about it."

This is true – he once asked me why I kept coming to him while I was still married to Ben, and I told him, not unkindly, that I didn't want to discuss it and, in any event, it was none of his business.

"Your reasons for sleeping with me are your reasons" he continued "and your reasons for staying married are your reasons too. I don't expect you to throw in your marriage for me, and let's face it, I am probably not a good bet."

He says this with good humour, but he does make a point.

"I think it would be a silly thing for me to do, to fall in love with you. Whatever your reasons for staying with Ben I am not the type of man that would be happy to wait in the wings for a bit of your attention."

I know that this is also true – Simon has always been open and direct with me and has never asked for anything more that the time I am able to give to him, just as I have never asked for anything more from him. I think we have always understood that he has his life, and I have mine, but occasionally they will overlap in all the right ways.

My next question baffles me almost as much as it baffles him.

"What would happen to us if you were to fall in love with someone else?" I ask.

He moves his head to look down on me and I raise my eyes to look up at him. He is smiling again.

"Well, I would have to tell her that I already love someone and have done for a very long time, and frankly, you've got dibs!"

I laugh at this, and he strokes my hair and I rest back down on his chest. I realise that I don't want to lose this man, but that I also don't want to have him either – perhaps that is because I would always be worried that I could not contain him, that I would always believe that he would want to be somewhere else with someone else.

Later after we have slept a little, he ties me up with his work tie that I bought him specifically for this purpose, and he fucks me on my knees with my head down on the bed and my wrists lashed behind me. I cum over and over and tell him then beg him to stop, to give me a break because I can't stand the ecstasy any more, but he doesn't – I shake and tremble with every orgasm and post-orgasm rush, and when he is finally done with me my muscles tremble with exhaustion. He unties my wrists and he and I fall back into bed, me laying happily on his chest with my arm over him and have a long and deep sleep. In the morning, before I leave to go to work, I ride on him hard and cum again with another shivering orgasm. We shower together in the hotel's exquisite bathroom, and kiss warmly and deeply before I go.

I reflect later that he never asked whether I love him – he just left that he loved me and that was that.

Becca is on today, and she has become my close friend, even more so since Sarah left a few weeks ago, my confidante and my co-conspirator – yesterday, as far as Ben is aware, I left work as usual then went for drinks and clubbing with Becca before staying at hers, when in fact I left work at lunchtime and only saw Becca for her to wink at me quickly as I was leaving. We had worked this plan out between us when I knew Simon was going to be in town.

She doesn't need to come over and ask how the night went, I am sure she can see it from my face ("and your walk" she says later) that I have had a good night. My pussy is sore but every time I think about it, it reminds me of the night I have had with Simon, and I know that as sore as I am I am going to finger myself mercilessly when I get home.

I finally give in to the uncomfortable reminders of him and text him at about 11am.

>I love you too xxx

He replies almost immediately:

>I know x

Ella

A few months later and Sepp had gone, back to France at first but then Kacper tells me that he heard a rumour that he had gone back to Poland with his tail between his legs, having been unable to make his life work anywhere else.

For a little while I missed him, and there were tears when he was packing, and I almost changed my mind and went with him. I did love him, I know that, but the life he wanted was not the life I wanted. He wanted a family and a wife at home to keep house, and I am sure that his leaving was precipitated by him not being able to get any work and having to be supported by his girlfriend. Sepp was no Roman when it comes to Polish men, but it must have hurt his feelings that he was being provided for, not being the provider.

And to be honest, for him to have a family with me we would have to have sex, something that I certainly had no time for. This wasn't helped for him by Anna who seemed to have a string of boyfriends home and between her and her men friends they seemed to have been having a wonderful time. Once or twice with the unrestrained noises coming from the room next door Sepp would turn to me and stroke my back or my shoulder, but I would pretend to be asleep and that would be that.

She once told me that she had only agreed to move in with me just so that she be able to have sex, because her place had been so horrible that she had never attempted to take a man there out of shame more than anything else. If those first few weeks were anything to go by, she was trying to make up for lost time, but unfortunately also trying Sepp's patience for staying in England.

Once Sepp had gone Anna seemed to slow down a bit, and I might see the same man two or three times rather than the absolute once it had been before. This was an enormous relief to me due to the number of times I would run into a complete stranger in my kitchen whilst I am half asleep and in nothing more than my 'oversized' pants (which Anna would still tease me about) and a vest. As time went on the overlaps between men also reduced until she was at the point of almost going steady with a ginger haired computer analyst called Gavin, when Alan entered her life.

To say entered her life is a bit of a stretch as she had been working for Alan for almost as long as she had been in the country – he was the boss of the parts export firm that she had been working for temporarily, and unsurprisingly proving to be an asset to the firm he had taken her on permanently. It was a job she was adept at and liked – a lot of her day was spent, apparently, charming the pants off French businessmen and suppliers on the continent to take this or that consignment, increase their orders or only offer the parts she could supply as exclusive deals. She was good at it, even if she didn't have much of an idea what it was she was actually selling. People responded well to her. I knew her well enough to know she wasn't being flirtatious, just charming, pleasant and helpful whilst at the same time selling company products.

People always responded well to Anna and as a result Alan's business had done very well out of her over the year that she had worked there.

Alan was single having never married, was in his mid-to-late thirties and, as I would expect from Anna, handsome. Gavin, I think, had been a bit of an anomaly and Anna's idea of trying to settle down with someone sensible – Alan seemed to have an all year tan whilst Gavin had been borderline unnaturally pale. Anna had been attracted to Alan immediately she saw him, apparently, but had never done anything about it assuming that he was already married, and I cannot imagine that Alan hadn't noticed Anna when she started working there. Like I have said before, she has a personality that can fill a room. Whilst Anna's moral compass did not extend to limiting the number of her lovers, I knew well that she would never have considered a relationship with a married man.

He had asked her out one day after a work's do, having, in his words, plucked up the courage to ask a younger woman if she would mind very much being seen out with an older man and she had accepted immediately, once she had assured herself that he was indeed, surprisingly, single. She had introduced him to me almost straight away, and I have to say that I liked him immediately. Yes, he was handsome, and yes, he was clearly quite well off – he drove a big grey car, I don't know things like makes and models, but it looked very impressive – he was charming too and of all the things I liked about him, it was his accent most of all.

Of all the things that I had not expected when I was coming to England it was that not everyone speaks the same way. I had expected...well, I don't know quite what I had expected but I had thought that all English people spoke in a nice flowing and gentle manner. I wasn't expecting the voices I had heard when I lived in Poland from old time movies and TV shows, but I had expected something...refined? It was an enormous disappointment to me to realise that no one spoke in the refined manner I had expected, and that there was an overuse in my view of profanity that I didn't like at all.

Alan spoke like I had expected all English people to speak. I could see why Anna liked him. On the one time I did run into him at our house whilst in my pants and vest he simply apologised and looked the other way whilst I grabbed my cereal and a coffee from the pot (which I noticed Alan had already brewed) and ran back up the stairs. It's not that he had ignored me, he had said good morning and drawn my attention to the coffee pot whose smell had enticed me from my bed in the first place, it's just that he politely looked the other way and didn't stare speechless and open mouthed like so many of Anna's boyfriends had done.

Thanks to Alan having his own home, a place outside of town with large gardens and that looked like a palace (according to Anna), the nocturnal disturbances from the room next door diminished too. In a way I almost missed them, a reminder that the house was empty of everyone but me. But then I have always been happy in my own company and didn't think about it too much.

For me, work was going very well. I had done several trainings and now had some qualifications in care work, and my colleagues were encouraging me to look for other senior jobs, not that they wanted me to leave, but they were keen for me to do well. I had certainly given it some thought and was looking around for another challenge, and to be honest the salary bump would be welcome too. Anna was still paying her fair share of the rent, but I had started to wonder how long it would be before she made the sensible decision to move into Alan's 'palace' with him. Anna must have known that I was thinking like this and had assured me, many times, that she had no intention of leaving me alone, but that did not give me any reassurance when I was lying in bed in and empty and quiet house.

It did give me plenty of time to think, though, and I promise myself on one of those dark and quiet nights that I would find a new job, one that stretched me a little more and paid me a little better, just in case I suddenly found myself having to meet the rent on my own.

Alina

I don't know quite when I would define Simon, Mr Holcroft, and I starting to see each other, or when I started to think about him as a romantic possibility – but I remember our first kiss well enough and maybe it was then. Not long after the incident with Christiana – the same week that Andrei came home with that hideous outfit for me – I had decided that I had had enough of being misused, and I could not risk another episode like that, so I decided that the only option I had was to leave Andrei and take Christiana and Mama with me.

The only problem was I knew no one other than the people I lived with and the people I worked with, and I didn't think that there were many in either group that had either the knowledge or the willingness to help me. After considering the options I realised that I had just one – take up Simon's offer of talking to him.

I thought I would ask him if he would mind meeting me after work one day – it took a lot of courage for me to go and ask, I am not used to asking anyone for help with anything. I must have gone to or past his office door four or five times before I finally knocked and went in. He looked up from what he was working on and there must have been something about my expression that immediately said I wasn't there for anything routine.

"You came to me," he said softly, sitting back in his chair and putting his pen down, "just tell me what I can do."

I am immediately unsure. I had thought that I would be in control here and just begin a sequence of events that would lead to my family being safe. I would arrange to meet with him and set out a plan, but I now realise I have no plan to set out. All I have is this man that I don't know very well and the sure knowledge that I cannot continue living with Andrei.

I think he sees me hesitate – unconsciously I think I even made half a step backwards to leave.

"Alina, come in, sit down – you're here for some help, right?"

I nod weakly.

He comes around from behind the desk and puts his hand on my back to gently propel me toward the other chair whilst he continues to close the door behind me. I sit in the chair, but I can feel the tension in me, I am perched awkwardly on the edge of the chair, stiff and upright and I have no idea where to put my hands.

He returns to the other side of the desk.

"How would you like to start?" he asks. I am not sure what he means, and he clearly sees that. "There is a story here, isn't there, one that is probably not very easy to relay in places, that has led you to coming into my office today because you needed someone to turn to, and out of all the people that you know I am your least worst option."

I look at the floor but nod – I have left my hair unsecured today and it falls past my face, which makes an effective screen if I need it.

"So – start at the beginning."

It is easier now that I am not looking at him – I do very broad-brush strokes about marrying Andrei, coming to England, learning the language, and then coming here. I skip over some things I am not prepared to talk about, like the sex, and how I always had some bad feelings about Andrei, but I talk about the gambling and drinking, and I tell him about how unhappy that makes me and how difficult it can be at home. I mention my daughter and Mama, but I am beginning to run out of steam without talking about the things that I don't want to talk about.

I splutter to a stop leaving an empty space in the air where it was filled with my words a moment ago – I haven't looked up since I started talking. I notice that there are tears dripping off the end of my nose and a tissue in my hand that, now I think about it, Simon handed me as I was talking. The silence is only broken by me sniffling and snorting.

"I'm…sorry" I say between sniffles.

"You have nothing to be sorry about – what on earth makes you think you have to apologise to me?"

"You didn't have to have all of that – I shouldn't have…"

"Shouldn't have what, Alina? Shouldn't have come to ask for help when you needed it? Shouldn't have made the decision to protect yourself and your family?"

I shrug my shoulders. I don't know what to say anymore. What I have held inside is now out there, in the open, exposed to the world and this one man. I dry my eyes and blow my nose – the tissue is black afterwards as my makeup has run. Seeing this acts almost like a reminder to pull myself together and I sit up and carefully wipe my eyes and face, and Simon offers me another tissue.

"I don't suppose you have a mirror, do you? I ask – he points to the back of the door where, of course there is, I recall there is a rectangular mirror hanging.

I get up and clean myself up a bit, then come and sit down again.

"Ok," he says, "to be fair there is only so much I can do as your manager." I nod and I begin to think that this was a terrible mistake. "I can give you any time off you need, I can probably find a few numbers that you can call for support – I can't make those calls for you, that will have to be you." He pauses and, in the space, I nod weakly again. I can see that he is looking at me in that way he has of looking straight through people.

"But what I think I can do, that you need, is to be someone that you can talk to about things as you do what you need to do and go through what you are going to have to go through." He scribbles a number down on a piece of paper. "Here, this is my personal number. Use it if you need it." I take it from his outstretched hand and put it straight in my pocket. "If you need someone to talk to, call me – any time, OK?" I nod weakly again, but this time throw in a smile too.

We don't talk more about Andrei and me but he changes the conversation to more general topics about the ward, the weather, general stuff, and when I feel ready to go back out to the ward I stand up and say that I had better get on with my duties. I then notice the time – I have been in the office for 45 minutes. I am shocked and hurriedly retreat to the door, thanking him as I go.

True to his word, 20 minutes later he emerges from the office and wordlessly hands me a printout of some phone numbers to call – a domestic violence helpline, women's refuge, housing helpline etcetera. I fold it up and put that in my pocket too. On my way home I pull my car over and transfer the numbers to my mobile and put Simon's number in, under the name Louise – well, that is one thing that she can do for me. I use the cigarette lighter in the car to set fire to the paper at the roadside before I go home.

When I get there things are quiet – no Andrei, but that is nothing unusual, when he does come home it is rarely before 10pm. I tell Christiana and Mama that I am tired and need a lie down, and I probably look it having had to wipe off my makeup earlier. Mama nods and grasps my hand to give it a squeeze then takes herself off to the kitchen to make something for her and Christiana for dinner.

In the quiet darkness of my bedroom I pull out my phone and make a couple of quiet calls. I am composed, compared to my earlier self, and tell Margaret, the nice sounding case worker at the domestic violence helpline everything – including the sex – in an almost detached way, like I am talking about a TV show or book. We are on the phone for almost an hour, and the call ends with several more numbers for me to call if I need them and a promise to call me back in a day or two, although I ask if I can call her rather than her calling me in case Andrei is here. She accepts that and gives me her extension number and tells me what hours she is working.

With that done I fiddle with my phone, clicking open the contact name 'Louise' and closing it again. Opening it and closing it. Finally, I type:

>Thank you

Simon writes back:

>No problem.

I leave it almost an hour before I send back:

>Can I talk to you after work sometime? Perhaps Thursday?

> No problem, I'll meet you at Costa at 4.30.

And that is how it starts – I text him a day and we meet up at the coffee shop and I unload and tell him all about what is happening with me. He sits and listens and always insists on buying the coffee. I tell him about the calls I have had, when I have been to appointments for support or housing, I sense check things with him (although he usually tells me that he is not the expert, the people whose job it is to know these things are and I need to listen to them). I tell Andrei that I have extra duties or something, but he doesn't care as long as I am home by the time he gets home.

And four weeks later I have a new place to move into – it isn't anything much, but it is mine and some distance away from where I lived – no, I survived – with Andrei. The last few weeks have taught me much, including have forced me to accept that I don't have to be a victim, and I can feel the old me, the me before I got married, the me that was strong and confident inside as well as out, the me that didn't have to put up a front all the time, coming back. It is like greeting an old and dear friend. I told Christiana and Mama the day before we were leaving – I had already told Andrei that the three of us were going to go on a shopping trip as I had a day off, and to not expect us home until later – and that they were to pack their things, just the things that they had to have, ready to go on the Saturday.

Andrei took my planned shopping trip as an excuse to be out all night from the Friday which gave us all some extra time to get what we needed, and by lunchtime we were gone, posting all our keys back through the letter box as we walked away from that place for the last time. Simon knew, of course, we had discussed it, so I was not surprised when I got a message from him that evening asking how it went and was everything OK. I sent back that it had gone better than expected and that Mama and I were having a glass of red wine – which we were, even though neither of us usually drink alcohol.

> I'm pleased to hear it – make sure you enjoy yourselves
>
> See you at Costa on Monday?
>
> Of course

We meet at the coffee shop and this time Simon lets me buy the coffee. He says that I had better get the decaf because I look like I am bouncing, and I can't remember the last time I felt like I had this much energy. He asks me to describe my new place, asks about schools for Christiana, and smiles at me the whole time, but then I feel like I am smiling so much the top of my head might fall off at any moment. I don't stop talking for the time we are there.

As we leave and are standing on the pavement outside I can't help but throw my arms around him and stand on tiptoes to kiss him on the cheek – he looks a little taken aback, but then smiles and kisses me on the cheek too, and even today, so much later and with so much else that has happened in our lives I remember that kiss, the first time I had had a kiss of genuine warmth from any man.

Alina (again)

People at work can see a difference in me. I smile more, I know that, but they start to look at me differently. I can see them trying to work out what is going on with me. Louise and I swap numbers (I move Simon's number under his real name) and begin talking more at work and we even meet up out of work. I feel like I am looking better too. At the supermarket or in the town I see plenty of men smiling at me, and why wouldn't they? It's nice to have the attention but that is all, thank you.

Simon and I meet up regularly still and, yes, we still share a warm kiss on the cheek when we separate. We have expanded our venues and sometimes will have lunch together or an evening meal out. I rarely pay, because he won't take money from a single parent, he says.

It is Louise that tells me that the rumour circulating the ward is that Simon and I are sleeping together. I can't help but roll my eyes at this – of course, in their mean and tiny minds the two people that they like the least must be sleeping together as this explains why both of us expect the rest of them to do their jobs. It also explains why he and I can have a conversation, even share a joke or a smile, whereas the rather simpler explanation that we have just got to know each other and can have a human interaction without having sex with each other. I can see their logic.

Simon's standing with the staff is not helped when Bernice is caught by a relative taking cash out of a patient's wallet and is dismissed on the spot by Simon. As the apparent number two in command (after the maintenance man) the consensus is that he should have given her a chance.

When Simon begins an investigation into the maintenance man – he tells me in confidence, even though we both know he shouldn't, that he found evidence that none of the maintenance schedules had been followed for months – he promptly goes off sick with 'work stress' – again, Simon told me – before resigning. Leaderless, the staff turn to ever more inventive ways of trying to prove Simon and I are an item, to the extent that one of the other nurses is caught listening outside Simon's office window when I am in there. His excuse is that he was just passing on his way from another part of the hospital and was taking a short cut to use the fire exit to re-enter the building.

He receives a stern rebuke not least of which because it isn't short, and he has left the fire door propped open so that he can get back in.

For a while it is an even more unpleasant work environment than before, but then some staff begin to realise which side their bread is buttered and pull their socks up, others, the more vocal ones, find other jobs and Simon replaces them with good people who do want to work for a living.

Bizarrely, this does push Simon and I closer together and we confide in each other more, but rarely in work – or on the shop floor as Simon refers to it – usually over a light lunch at Cote. I am comfortable around him; I start to share with him some of the worst about my ex-husband (a divorce is well underway) and we talk about everything and nothing. As far as I can tell he is never dishonest with me. He even tells me about a strange on-again and off-again relationship he had for a while which even carried on through his brief marriage. I can remember being less shocked about this than I would have thought that I would be. He tells me he still loves this woman in a way that is hard to quantify, although he doesn't think that they will be coming back together any time.

I don't know what compels me to make the first move with him – it is during the winter, and the snow has been so bad that the hospital has offered some on call rooms to staff if they need. I can't think of anything worse than staying in an on-call room, and I ask Simon if he would mind if I stayed at his, a flat within a reasonable walking distance from the hospital, even in deep snow. Of course, he doesn't mind and gives me a spare key – he won't be coming back to the flat until much later, if at all, as staff struggle to get in for the night shift. He tells me the spare bed is made up, where to find towels and things, and says to call me if I have any problems. I'm sure I won't – I have been to his flat a few times and know the layout well enough. I call Mama and tell her I am fine but to not wait up for me as I will be staying here - I don't tell her that I am staying in a man's flat.

I leave a little later than usual – staff make it in but are a bit late, and I wave goodbye to Simon as I leave. He is in his dark blue nursing tunic rather than his usual suit, covering the nursing until more support arrives.

At his almost the first thing I do is take a shower to warm up – I am frozen to the bone after walking here, and then walk around his flat wrapped in a towel looking at things he has, the photos he has on the mantle, opening drawers and cupboards – the sort of thing anyone would do left alone in someone else's home. The whole place *feels* like Simon, it smells like him, it is him. I am unable to contain my curiosity and open his bedroom door – there is a large, and messily unmade bed that looks like someone has just rolled out of it. He has a built-in wardrobe and I open the doors to see rows of neatly ironed shirts. These smell even more like him.

I take one out – a blue striped shirt that I recognise – and slip it on letting my towel fall to the floor. On me it is like a nightgown – well, I hadn't brought any night clothes with me, so I keep it on. I gather up the towel and hang it on the heated towel rail in the bathroom.

He has very little in his fridge except Budwisers – so I make myself a little pasta, open a bottle of Bud and eat and drink curled up on the sofa with the TV on, although I couldn't tell you what the programme was, before taking myself to the spare bed. It's big and it is comfortable and warm and before long I must have fallen asleep.

I am woken by an unfamiliar noise a couple of hours later and I realise I hear keys in the door – it must be well past midnight, so I put a light on and open the bedroom door to check. It is Simon coming in, shivering and wet through as he shucks off his coats that is covered in fresh snow – I hadn't realised that it was snowing again. He turns and sees me framed in the bedroom doorway.

"Oh, hello" he says "Well, I am not sure that I can wear that again as it looks a lot better on you."

I am not sure what he means then remember I am in his shirt.

I start to apologise, but instead I cross over to him and place my hand flat over his heart and rest my head against his chest. He feels cold and I shiver; he hesitates before he puts his arm around my shoulders and holds me to him and rests his cheek on my head. We stand there for a moment by the front door before I tighten my hand into a fist to grab the material of his tunic and pull him down toward me. I kiss him on the mouth then pull away to look at his eyes. There is hesitation there, but then he gently cradles my head in his hand and leans down to kiss me back.

The kiss is deep and passionate – and I can feel his passion rising in him.

"You're cold" I say, "let's go and get warm, shall we?"

I lead him by the hand back to the spare room and I take his cold and damp clothes off him in between kisses on the lips and on his fingertips. The wet clothes get dropped on the floor and before long he is naked sitting on the bed I was sleeping in a few minutes before. His passion is indeed risen, but I can see him shiver a little still. I lift up the shirt a little and sit across his lap and guide him into me to an accompanying mutual gasp. There is no urgency here, I am going to take my time with this man and hold him here for as long as I need to. I have my arms around his neck, and he slides his cold hands up my bare thighs to grasp my buttocks. His hands provide a slow rhythm for me, I ease myself back and forth on him, kissing that beautiful mouth, that beautiful face, looking into those beautiful brown eyes, our breathing becoming harder. I have never felt like this, never felt like I want this to go on forever, never felt the pressure building inside me. Involuntarily I can feel my hips beginning to thrust against him with more urgency, but his hands bring me back to a slower rhythm again, much to my frustration.

"More" I sigh.

"No" he says between deep kisses.

I need this. I need it more than I have ever needed anything or anyone.

I take my arms from around his neck and push him back sharply, leaning forward over him to place my hands on his shoulders. I gasp as this makes him go even deeper into me and he does too, and again my hips seem to want to work to their own rhythm. I am rocking back and forth on his manhood, letting the full sum of him slide in and out of me. This time he is not resistant to my urgency, and his hands grip my backside so tightly. I want his mouth on mine so badly, I need his kisses, and I lean down to have what I need.

"Îmi place atât de mult" I whisper.

The end, when it comes, is unlike anything I have experienced. The pressure seems too great to bear until it explodes in me and all I have comes crashing out of me in waves of pure pleasure. He cries out and I know that he has joined me in the moment as he shudders beneath me. I feel like I have nothing left, that I am empty, that I have poured myself out into him and left myself a void and I collapse down on top of him, his manhood still deep inside me.

We lay like that until our breathing returns to normal, and I don't notice when I fall asleep.

We awaken some time later – he is still inside me – and I think it is the cold that wakes me up. I stir and kiss him again and climb off, letting him come out of me but not without feeling a little thrill as he does so. He flicks off the light and climbs into the bed, then holds the duvet up as an invitation that I gladly accept, and I slide in beside him and rest my head on his shoulder.

He kisses my forehead and whispers "Goodnight". I smile into the darkness and snuggle myself into him as close as I can, and in no time, we are asleep again.

Dee

I think that Ben is getting suspicious. Fairly recently he was, well, for Ben, pretty forceful about putting tracking software on both of our phones. Just in case, he had said, but not just in case of what. He had dressed it up as being an impressive new technology and as an added safety measure, but I am pretty sure that he had other reasons.

In fairness, he does.

Simon and I are still seeing each whenever we are both free, and I use any host of excuses to be able to spend time with him. Sometimes we just have lunch together, or a drink after work – this isn't always easy as he doesn't live or work in London but is here often enough on work matters for us to be able to meet up.

I always wear something pretty for him, and I always leave my knickers at home or slip them off in the toilets at work to put them into my handbag – I love sitting beside him in a pub with his hand up my skirt, trying hard not to look like I am cumming from what he is doing to my clit, or beside him in the car with his fingers inside me as he drives, me writhing and cumming in the passenger seat. In between seeing him I think about him all the time and when I do it is all I can do not to have my fingers in my pussy. I wank myself off two or three or four times most nights – sometimes with his help by text as he tells me what he wants me to do – and I send him naked pictures of myself when I am done. Once I even shaved my pussy for him and sent him pictures of that, and even though it was a little red and raw couldn't keep from having my fingers in it – it felt so good, I was making myself cum even more than usual.

I bought a dildo and a vibrator, then an anal plug to play with at home which I have to hide carefully. When Simon and I are together one of my favourite things is when he fucks me in the ass, sometimes with my wrists tied behind my back, sometimes not. The first time hurt a little but then made me feel like my head was going to explode. I bought him a paddle to bring with him when we meet up, and more than once my ass has been stinging for days with the sweet reminder of Simon and how he plays my body like an instrument. To him I am his willing plaything, I want him to own me, to make me tremble and shake, to beg him for an orgasm or, more often, to beg him for respite – a respite that I know I don't want, and that I know I am not going to get.

Becca revels in the stories I tell her of our meetings – more than once telling me how hot it is, and even how hot it makes her feel. I think she is living vicariously through me and does everything she can to help me make my meetings with Simon.

This latest development, with the phone tracking, is a problem though.

Ben knows that Becca lives in Hackney, so if he sees me in a hotel in Islington, he is going to have his suspicions, if that's what they are, confirmed.

The next night I have with Simon after this takes Becca's conspiracy to a whole new level – she suggests that we swap phones, and that she will take mine to her house, and I will take hers with me. Then if there are any calls or texts she can let me know, on her phone, that I need to call Ben or that I can call her and tell her what to send back in a text message. Then we just swap back in the morning. If I have to call Ben, I can do it from her phone and just pretend that there is some sort of signal or battery problem with mine. Any concerns I have about this plan, Becca seems to have an answer.

As it turns out there weren't any texts or calls for us to deal with, and in any event if there had been I was far too busy getting a thoroughly decent fucking to be looking at Becca's phone, anyway.

We swap back our phones in the morning at work with a promise from me that I will relate the more explicit details of my night with Simon later over lunch, although when we do meet up, we end up talking about Becca's confession.

"I have to tell you something", she says almost immediately, "and I am sorry, but I just couldn't resist!"

"Resist what?"

"Looking through your phone, of course! I have been up half the night reading your messages and playing with my clit so much I thought the damn thing was going to fall off. Honestly, I have never read anything so hot in all my life."

I don't know what to say, so I say nothing.

"I looked through your pictures too" she says and has the decency to look a little embarrassed at this.

"Becca!!"

I do feel ambivalent about what she has just confessed to me. Obviously, being called hot by anyone that has seen you naked (except for your doctor, I suppose) is a good thing but I had had no intention of my work colleague ever seeing me naked.

"I couldn't help it! I wanted to see what gets him so hot and bothered! And, oh my God, why didn't you say what a hot bod you're packing under that tunic!"

She is smiling at me and now I can't help but acknowledge the compliment and smile back. But it is clear that she is not finished yet.

"To be honest, that made me hornier than the texts. I came all over you at least twice last night."

It had never occurred to me to think that Becca might be gay nor that our friendship might be something else, but as it turns out she I don't think she is, and I don't think that it is, either.

"It's not like I am a lezzer or anything, but Jeez, what a bod."

I can't do much except look at her with, what I am sure, is a slightly stunned expression on my face, and I shake my head at her, and then promise to myself and to her that no matter what she is not having my phone unsupervised again.

I talk to her about the night and give her the details that she clearly craves, but all too quickly lunch is over and talking about my night has made me as horny as fuck again. There is nothing I can do about this, nor would want to do about this at work, until I get home, though, and it is a frustrating wait which only adds to the feeling of need.

Becca texts me at about 6.30 to let me know I have made her cum again, and I text her back to tell that a) she is a dreadful human being and I wish I didn't know her and b) she is about twenty minutes behind me. She sends me a kissy face icon leaves it at that.

I can't keep my promise to Becca, though – two weeks later whilst I am bent over a desk being spanked in another hotel room, I am acutely aware that I have Becca's phone in my bag, and she has mine at her house.

I know this is unsustainable though – it nags away at me. The guilt, of course, but that isn't the main issue. I don't like having to use my friends – and I have used pretty much all of my friends at one time or another, whether they know it or whether they don't. Ben asks more questions than he used to, and he can't have helped but notice that I always seem too tired for sex or that on the rare occasions when we do have sex that it is entirely unsatisfactory for me, no matter how often I tell him it isn't necessary for me to cum to be having a nice time. He starts talking about children, something that I definitely don't want – I determined a long time ago that I am far too selfish to want children, I want nice things and nice holidays and to be the centre of attention, not bring horrid children into the equation.

However, what breaks the cycle, what disrupts my relationship with Simon is not my friends, it is not being found out and it is not having had enough of what I get from him.

It is Simon.

He calls me one day – and he never calls – to tell me that he wants to see me about something important and he is coming up to London tomorrow, can I see him? I agree, naturally, and we meet up for lunch, but don't get anywhere near the café before he tells me what this meeting is about.

"It's not enough" he says, and at first, I think he is talking about the amount of sex we are having, but I can see that that is not it.

"When we met – when we met in that God awful training – I didn't know a thing about you – and by the time of car park… you remember the car park?"

I nod.

"Well, even then, I knew next to nothing about you. I was shocked when you told me you were going for a wedding dress fitting, and I thought that nothing could ever come of us."

He has stopped walking now, so I turn to stand in front of him. He takes this as a sign to hold both of my hands in both of his.

"The more time went on, and the less we talked about everything, I took us for just being… well, fuck buddies or something, I guess…" He's squeezing my hands, but not hard.

"I want more from you, Dee – I want to be able to go home to you and do stupid things like walk hand in hand with you down the street without worrying that someone you know might see us."

I stand there, in the street, looking at him slightly open mouthed.

"I remember taking you for that walk, when we walked down the street holding hands, like it was real or something. It felt real, but I remember looking into your face and… well, it didn't look like you were feeling the same way, and now –

the truth is that I want the real from you, Dee. I want real – I want, well, real." He ends lamely, and drops my hands as his hands fall to his sides and he awkwardly shuffles with them until he puts them into his pockets.

There might have been a time a long time ago when I would have thrown in everything I have with Ben and tried for a relationship with this man – but if there was it would have to have been long before that meeting the car park on my way to a dress fitting. I think about that moment now and realise that that was the last chance I had to change the course of my life and my marriage, that meeting my Mum that day and getting fitted for a wedding dress was more important than the man stood in front of me then, and now, and I know deep in my heart that that moment has set the tone for our whole relationship, and even, in some respects, the tone for today. I am looking at him shuffling awkwardly, his gaze not meeting mine for a moment, until he lifts his head to look at me.

I think he can see me hesitating and he steps forward and takes both of my hands in his again.

"I can't do that, Simon." I say, through choked breath – the dawning on me of the gravity of that chance meeting so long ago is suddenly a heavy weight to bear, and I feel like the whole of that weight is on my chest, preventing me from breathing properly.

"I know – but I wanted you to know that I do love you, Dee, and I want to see where that love goes or make the decision that I have to move on." His voice is low, quiet and tender. Now my head is bowed because I don't want to look at him right now, and he is trying to duck low enough to look into my face. After a moment I raise my head and look straight into his eyes.

"So, you're giving me an ultimatum, leave Ben or it's over?" I am suddenly angry with him, and I can tell that my tone as acid edges to it. I know inside that this is misdirected, but I can feel a sense of loss stretching back to that car park, and a scene that I can see so vividly.

"No Dee, I'm telling you that you made your decision a long time ago to stay with Ben and I respect that – now I have to make a decision that is right for me, and I am asking you to respect that too. I can't do this anymore." He is still holding my hands, but I am not holding his. I can feel myself trembling a little, but with which one of the particular mix of emotions I have at the moment, I am not sure.

I don't know what to say, on the pavement on a hot day in London. I am angry, I am sad, I am fighting the urge to scream at him and to kiss him, and at the same time I am seeing the logic of what he is saying to me, especially when he adds:

"Tell me honestly that you would even consider leaving Ben for me." And I know that I wouldn't.

He lets go of my hands and steps back a pace, his hands returning to his trouser pockets.

Suddenly he is staggering back, away from me. I am unsure why until I realise that my hand is clenched into a fist and hurts – I look at it and then at him in some disbelief, a disbelief that I can see that he shares. I slap him, hard, open-handed this time, right across the face. He stands there and takes it, unmoving, the sound of it seemingly echoing back from the buildings. Even in London, people turn to look. He doesn't even reach up to where his face is very clearly reddening.

I am shaking, my eyes blurry, tears coming, as though it was me that had been hit. My anger, such that it was, is spent – or at the very least buried under so many competing thoughts and emotions that I can't feel it as acutely, and I can now feel a throbbing pain in my hand. Then, unbelievably, he holds his arms apart slightly and I step into the space created and put my arms around him, for what I start thinking might be the last time. He holds me, just holds me, and then he leans down and kisses me on the cheek.

And then he lets go of me and he walks away. He just walks away. I watch his back as he disappears into the crowd, thinking that he will turn back, but he doesn't.

Ella

True to her word Anna carries on paying her share of the rent, but I seem to see less and less of her. The relationship with Alan is clearly becoming a serious one, and I can see the changes in Anna as a result – she is going out less frequently, although we still have the pub together, and when she does go out with me and can see that she is, well, less predatory than she was. There is no more sizing up of men coming into the bar, except in a more casual way when we have been on the subject of my love life, which is non-existent.

Anna always seems incredulous that I don't miss having a sex life, but the truth is there was very little to miss. Sepp and I did have sex a few times, but it felt uncomfortable and wrong. She was outraged one night when I let slip that I didn't think that Sepp had ever seen me naked and tried to get me to explain how that was even possible.

The thing is that although I am a few years older, I know that I am still that tall, skinny, flat chested, slightly awkward girl. As Anna would be the first to tell me, I don't move with either grace or style and I have zero fashion sense. I try to tell her that the clothes I wear I wear because they are comfortable and practical. I tell her I keep my hair short because it takes less time to get ready in the morning. I tell her I don't wear makeup because I work every day with old sick people, not in a disco. I tell her that I like my pants because they cover a lot, are comfortable and keep me warm (what warmth benefit can she possibly get from some of her pants?) and then she will invariably tell me off for calling them 'pants' ("when is 'pants' ever a sexy word?").

But I know that it is more than just makeup, haircuts and clothes. Yes, there is the practicality argument about how I dress but I know that I am, and I always will be, the kind of person that most people will look past to look at the Annas, or the Sabines, of this world. It is just how things are, and I am not jealous that they get the attention that suits them, I would rather be let alone anyway. Oh, I know that I have complained about my empty house when Anna is away, but that is not for want of company, I know it is in dread for my security – I still think that Anna will move out to live with Alan and then I will have to make the changes I need so that I can survive. I would hate to leave my home here but if I had to, I would.

Bearing this in mind, I am bothered when Anna seems suddenly more secretive and I don't see her for over a week, whereas I would usually see her every couple of days at the least, usually as she comes home to load the washing machine. I try to shake off the feeling that there is more change in the air, but I can't, so the announcement that Anna is moving out doesn't come as a surprise, although what follows does.

I am on the sofa reading when I hear the keys in the door – I don't leap up, but I do look toward the hallway to wait for Anna to emerge into the living room. However, she does not appear straight away, and I can hear movement of something heavy and, perhaps, another voice? Not Alan's, and hushed, and my interest is piqued.

I have got as far as uncrossing my legs and have one foot on the floor to get up to investigate when Anna finally emerges.

"Hey you"

"Hey yourself – sounded like you were moving furniture out there"

"Yes, well, about that…" she is looking down at her hands, a sure sign that she has bad news "…I have to tell you that I have decided to move out. I'm moving in with Alan. And, well, I think we might even get married." She is speaking in a rush, and as she says the last bit, she looks up at me with a half-hopeful and half-ecstatic expression, an uncertain smile on her lips.

That is not the surprise though.

"Congratulations!" I say to hear, and now I get up from the sofa to throw my arms around her and hug her tightly. She is clearly relieved at this reaction and hugs me back.

"Nothing official yet" she adds, pointing to a vacant ring finger "although it's going really well and I am practically living with him anyway, so it seemed to make sense to move in officially." She seems to be reading my mind because she adds "and I have made sure you'll be OK too."

I look at her quizzically – has she found me a rich husband or something to move in with?

No.

Anna signals to the hallway, and I realise that there has been someone standing there for the last couple of minutes way back by the door. Tentatively they step forward into the living room, looking more nervous than I have ever seen her, and clutching at the handles of a holdall in both hands in front of her.

It's Grazyna.

I burst into tears and grab hold of her, squeezing so tightly I think I might burst her, and after a moment she drops her holdall (on my foot, but no matter), flings her arms around me and squeezes me back. There are tears in her eyes too and we stand like that for a minute or so before I look up to where Anna was. She is sitting on the arm of the armchair looking at as both with a smile on her face that I know so well from the many times she has plotted and made plans for me that have worked out.

"Oh, you two know each other?" she says, so I slap her on the arm playfully, then wipe my nose and my eyes on the back of hand.

"How? Why?" I manage to splutter, looking back and forth between the two of them.

The How, I realise, I have worked out in my head quickly, apart from a couple of minor details. Anna speaks to Sabine, Sabine speaks to Mama, so when Mama's special girl wanted to come to England it would been Sabine that brokered the deal to give Anna the opportunity she needed to move on with her own life. Grazyna (who wants me to call her Grace now that she is in England) and Anna confirm this over the next few minutes. The Why takes much longer, and cups of tea, then later wine, tears, and tissues.

Grazyna

He would never have said so, but Ella leaving had a profound effect on Father. On Mama it was there for the world to read on her – she grieved as though Ella had died, as though some cruel twist of fate had torn her from her breast and there was a finality to it. I think that Mama believed that she would never see her again, but clung on to the hope that she would, and so her grief lessened to the point of being able to be borne easier, but never to the point of acceptance, let only relief or happiness.

For me, her leaving had come as a shock – I always supposed that I would be the one to leave first, although in my case married to a wealthy, and hopefully handsome, husband. I was, we all knew, the pretty one who would secure a husband that would provide for me and our inevitable children that I would raise. That was how it had been supposed to go.

Father had nearly always provided everything for me that I wanted – money for dresses, hair, makeup, whatever I needed – and when he didn't it would only take a sad look that I perfected long before my teens to get what I wanted in the end. I knew I was his special girl and Ella had always known that she wasn't – so she would have been as surprised as I was to see the change in him.

Never much one for talking, Father became more sullen than usual. He took his sullenness out on the men more than once, there were days when Mama and I could hear his roaring voice from the orchard as someone was berated for some minor issue. He targeted one of the younger men most of all, a man – well a boy really – called Tomasz, because there was a rumour circulating that he had been having sex with Ella for months before she left. If you want my opinion, he wasn't the type, he was by all accounts too quiet, too boyish – but rumours are not known for being true, just believable enough to sound true. Tomasz didn't take it for long, though and left a few weeks after Ella did, taking a black eye with him, if rumour is to be believed.

He and Mama barely talked – the house seemed quiet as a grave as I would lay in my bed at night, listening to nothing but the wind, or the rain, or the creaking of the house – there was only one fewer of us, but the house felt so empty without there being human voices to break the curse of silence. For someone who had been so quiet when they were here, Ella's absence had taken away much more than I would have thought that she had added.

As I said, I had always been the one expected to leave first, and the oppressive silence of that house made me think more and more that it was about time I did, and the job I had had for myself since I was a teenager – that of finding a husband – I set about anew.

To my eternal misfortune, the target I gave myself was a friend of my Father's, Constantin. Constantin was a little younger than my Father but not by much – and what I knew of him was scant at best. He seemed well off, always bringing a gift of flowers for Mama when he would come to dinner and a bottle of something dark and red for Father which they would always finish between themselves long after the rest of the household had retired to bed. For a long time, I have known the effect I have on men, and I can recognise the look that they get in their eyes when they are looking at me, usually out of the side of their eye, but Constantin was bolder – he would stare with a smile on his face and nod appreciatively whenever I was in the room. He would always greet me like he did Father and Mother, with a kiss on each cheek, but I always felt he would hold me tighter and longer than he did either of them. He would give me compliments all the time, and joke with Father about taking me off his hands if he wanted. Of course, I would smile politely at this, after all, appreciative attention is attention, isn't it? And I enjoyed attention.

So, it was an easy and an obvious choice. He had started coming over much more often since Ella had left ("Supporting the family through a difficult time" he had said) – wealthy, liked by my Father, clearly interested, and to be fair to him quite a handsome man too. So, I started to make my play for him – those kisses of greeting I started kissing him back too. Instead of being held I would put my arms around him and hold him too. Instead of turning away I would look back when I noticed him looking at me and smile as warmly as I could. Before long there were signs that it was working – along with flowers for Mama, and a bottle for

Father, Constantin would arrive with a scarf for me, or a small bottle of perfume, or a brooch. I noticed the jokes to Father stopped, although to be fair the mood was barely one for jokes at the best of times, and this was not the best of times.

I do not know what discussions Father and Constantin had whilst emptying that bottle of dark red liquor, nor when they had it, but perhaps a year after Ella left, I was sitting at the kitchen table whilst Mama told me that her and Father (although how much contribution she had really made I would never be sure of) were to arrange a marriage between Constantin and me. It was not presented as an option, but I had been working on this for some months and knew that this is what I wanted.

Ella was not mentioned at all, and I can remember wondering why, with there being a palpable absence, Mama and Father – well, Father, really – had made the decision to empty the house further. The only reason I can come up with is that this had always been the plan for me, and Ella was gone – there was nothing that her leaving should be allowed to impact on their plans for me. Ella had never been part of that plan, the absence of someone who was never part of the plan should not change it, but I did wonder what kind of an impact an even emptier house would have on Mama and Father.

The wedding was everything that I had dreamed of – I had some many beautiful photographs of the day; everyone was there, and I had my dream dress – the train was twenty feet long, and the dress itself the purest white silks, lace, and pearls. Mama cried, of course, Father even managed to smile for the day. Constantin paid for it all – he was the centre of attention from his peers, my father included, circling around him with drinks and ribald humour. We opened the dancing together and I danced and danced, with Constantin, with our friends, with my father and with Mama. Constantin even bought me a white BMW as my wedding present which waiting for me as we left the reception.

Just like Father had wanted, Constantin took over the running of the farm – or rather, paid for someone to come and do it – so that Father could return to the orchards that he loved so much and leave the management of things to someone else. On the few occasions when I visited the farm and saw the men working there, there was a look of deference in their eyes that I had not had before – not only the boss' daughter, but now Constantin's wife. They would barely raise their heads to look at me.

I liked it.

The marriage itself, I did not.

I had heard of the honeymoon period, of course, which I had read about and that my girlfriends had talked about, and ours lasted just slightly longer than the length of the honeymoon itself. When we came back, we had a little time to be a newly married couple, did the family visits to my parents and to his mother, but very shortly Constantin was back to work and I was left at home with nothing to do but clean house, cook dinners and have sex with Constantin whenever he wanted – all of which were mundane tasks that I could take no pleasure from at all.

We would only go out together if there was somewhere that he wanted to be with me on his arm, and my function was to smile and look pretty whilst he stood in circles with his business contacts talking, drinking, and laughing. In fairness to begin with this was exciting being taken to expensive restaurants or colourful parties, but soon the food began to taste bland, and the colours paled, and the smile I wore felt more like it was fixed on.

It took less than two months for the physical relationship to all but stop. All too frequently Constantin would come home late, long after I had gone to bed, and get into the bed without a word and fall asleep, rise early in the morning, and have no time for conversation before being back out to work. I had, and still have, no idea what he did for work, all I know is he dressed smartly, and made good money.

I started visiting the farm more often, but got the distinct impression that this was no longer my place, interestingly from Mama more than anyone – she was colder than I was used to, she would busy herself with the housekeeping rather than sit and talk with me, and she would say things like "I won't keep you, you must be busy with a home of your own" as she made clear that it was time for me to leave.

I had never felt more alone. I barely spoke to anyone in those months – I would go for coffee with my girlfriends and tell them how wonderful married life was and shy away from the details that they wanted to hear, I could not bring myself to reveal how isolated I was, nor appear to have failed so completely in their eyes. I could see they were envious, I had wealthy husband, new car and clothes, some money to spend, so why they think I had everything that they could ever want?

After six months or so I tried to have a conversation with Constantin about starting a family – which at this point would have to have been a miraculous conception – but when I finally got him to have the discussion he gave a lengthy and reasoned argument why now was not the right time, which included finances, his workload, needing to spend more time together and getting to know each other better – which he assured me would be as soon as the impact his work had on his homelife settled down a bit – all sensible and rational reasons that boiled down to this was not happening, not now and not soon.

I noticed that I started to put on weight – so did Mama although I suspect she thought it was a pregnancy considering how her face fell when I started exercising and lost the weight again, and more. If there is a positive, it is that I became fitter than I have ever been as I took up jogging – naturally with nothing but the best running shoes and outfits that I could buy. I began to get appreciative looks in the street, men would turn their heads as I jogged by (once or twice followed by a sharp word from their wife or girlfriend) which always made me feel good.

I thought that this would help make me look good for when Constantin came home, so I would take special care and effort to try and attract him into spending time with me, but all too often I was fast asleep and only barely aware when he got home or when he left. If it was early enough for me to be awake, I am still not certain that he even noticed me anymore. It was never like it was when I lived at home – there I felt that he wanted my attention, sought it, played for it, but now I feel like I am just an accepted object in his home, like the sofa or the toaster, something smart and shiny and sits there looking smart and shiny and barely being used.

This was the start of a dawning realisation of Constantin wanted out of life – he desired things, so he went and got them, then once he had them, he no longer desired them. His home, his furniture, his status and now his wife. I had wondered why Constantin had not been married before and now I understood – women he had desired had been a short-term passion that had evaporated the moment he had acquired them. I wondered often if that was what kept him working so hard and so long, always desperate to acquire the next goal, the next target, and forgetting about them the moment he had them. I felt foolish for courting his attention, perhaps if I had known better, I would have realised I was just another acquisition, and then I realised that I was never the acquisition he sought, he wanted my father's business, and it just so happened that he could obtain a pretty wife at the same time as securing his business interests.

I began to fear for Father and especially for Mama, believing that at any moment Constantin would snatch their home and their lives out from under them, but in time realised that that was not his style, Constantin wanted to possess, not destroy. He had a foothold in the farm, but it wasn't him there running the business, it was a man he paid to do it, and when it came to me, I was clearly his possession, but he had never treated me badly, he was just indifferent to me – which was almost worse.

My Father's business was a tiny trophy, I was the free gift with every purchase, just like a shiny toaster, my family and I were just another thing to be possessed and to be forgotten about.

Still, though, I stuck by Constantin and the marriage – what else could I do? This was what I had been in training for since I was young, made to look pretty, ready to be the wife of a successful man. I felt that I was missing out on the only other part of my prescribed role, that of producing a family – but it is more than a little difficult to do that on your own. Sure, I could have the attention of a man if I wanted it – the looks in the street told me that – but I only had one job left to do and that was to be a wife.

I worked hard at that – I kept the house immaculate, I kept myself in good shape, I went to the social events with

Constantin and smiled, laughed and discreetly made myself absent in all the right places.

None of which filled the vacuum left by the lack of a relationship with my husband, or the absence of a family to care for. More and more I started to think about Ella, of course I missed her, but I began to think about what she had done, and mostly about how brave she had been to leave behind everything that she knew for a better life for herself. How, out of everything that we had at home, the one thing she had taken with her was the photo of me with Mama on the beach, whilst she was still little. I began to envy that courage, wishing I had the strength, missing my little sister more acutely than I had ever.

As I had been living more and more in this vacuum, I had been spending more time with Mama and the coldness she showed my when I was first married began to thaw – I think she saw that this is not what I wanted, and not what she wanted either, out of this marriage. I have been able to talk to her about the loneliness and emptiness I feel, she knows how unhappy I have been and for such a long time. She knows that all the money, cars and nice houses in the world do not make up for a lack of the comfort you can only get from a loving family. She will hug me warmly when I arrive and even more so when I leave.

We talk sometimes about Ella – and Mama misses her too – and it is she that suggests that I should speak to Sabine. She does it in a cautious, almost casual way, right after we have been speculating on what Ella has been up to, all these years. Mama says less than she knows, I think, and despite me having had no news on Ella since she left the suggestion is that Mama has been keeping tabs on her youngest, and, of course, Sabine has been the link.

It takes me a few days to take Sabine's number from Mama and nearly a month after that to actually make the call. Sabine is ecstatic to hear from me, she asks question after question about how I am, what I have been doing, what new clothes are in fashion – anything and everything except anything at all about marriage or Constantin. Mama has clearly prepared the ground well. I ask her if she has heard anything from Ella. It is like opening a floodgate. I hear about everything from her turning up at the vineyard, footsore, filthy, half-starved and exhausted, through leaving for England with a boyfriend that didn't last (which she knew it wouldn't, apparently, "but girls have to make their own mistakes"), to now living on her own.

"You two make a pair" she says.

"What do you mean?"

"Both of you, made your way and now find yourselves alone". This is the first reference she has made to knowing anything about the state of my marriage to Constantin. "Sisters stick together, you know, and you two are more alike than either of you would like to believe".

I stay silent for a moment, a silence that Sabine fills.

"You should go and see her, perhaps stay a while".

And that was that. Sabine suggested that she put me in contact with Anna, who thought the best thing in the world would be to come over and to keep me coming over a secret from Ella until I arrive. There are a few mores calls and we are all talking like this is just going to be an extended visit, and this is what I tell Constantin – who is entirely indifferent – but in my mind this is my chance to find the strength to take a brave step of my own, to find a life for myself rather than one set out for me. I think Sabine knows this too, but it is never discussed openly.

A few weeks later I am on a plane to Gatwick to meet up with Anna. I bought a return ticket because it will show on the credit card statement, but I have no intention of using it. I am done with being alone with nothing but four walls for company. This is my 'Ella' moment.

I just hope that she will be pleased to see me.

Alina

In a way, very little changes. Simon and I still meet up, sometimes out, sometimes in, and I look forward to the times when I know I am going to see him away from work. Of course, the people that thought we were having sex are now right, but I don't think that there is any change in how either of us behave that adds any certainty to those suspicions. He didn't take back his spare key after that night, come to think of it, he never even asked for it, and occasionally if I leave work a little before him, I will go to his flat and make myself a coffee and relax on his sofa until he gets in. He never seems surprised to see me, not even the first time I was there, even though I can't recall us ever having a conversation about meeting at the flat after work. We don't always end up in bed – more usually when I drop round in this way, I will just make him a tea when he gets in, we will talk about this and that, then I will go home – but never leaving before sharing a kiss with him.

I am advised by the domestic abuse worker not to rush into things with someone new – apparently, it is not uncommon after 'escaping' (her word, not mine) to rush straight into another relationship, good or, more frequently, bad. We communicate for a few weeks, but I think she can tell that I am settled and happy – and I have no unpleasant encounters from Andrei in this time either, except for a couple of offensive text messages that tell me how worthless I am, how I will come crawling back, how he can find three more like me on any street corner and so on. I block his number.

I do not tell the social worker about Simon though.

As far as I am aware, to begin with no one else knows about us – I don't ask him explicitly whether he has told anyone about us, and I certainly don't, but after some weeks I confide in Mama and tell her that I have a boyfriend and that I would like her to meet him. I am not sure what possesses me to talk to Mama about him, but I am glad that I do – she smiles and looks pleased and asks me if he is a good man.

I tell her that he is.

Simon is a little surprised when I ask him to come to dinner at my house but then looks pleased and accepts straight away. On the day itself Mama and I prepare dinner for us, and Mama is much more fussy than usual, pretty much taking over the cooking of everything and repeatedly telling me to worry less about the food and to make sure I look my best. At first, I am not sure why she is so invested in this dinner but then I realise that as much as I have seen a change in me, she must have seen it too and I ask her about this.

"I cannot remember the last time you were so happy", she tells me. "I have known for a long time that you have found a man to make you happy, and if he makes you happy, he makes me happy too. We will look after him together, OK?"

All I can think to do is to hug her warmly, and then do as I am told and leave the preparation to her whilst I get ready.

I have chosen a night when Christiana is staying at a friend's house so that Simon doesn't have too much to deal with all at once and to leave Christiana in the dark for now – I don't know where this relationship is going, and she has already had too much change to deal with to have more. I spend longer in the bath than usual, and it is Mama banging on the door that wakes me from the half-sleep I am having with a reminder that there is only an hour to get ready, as though I need more than ten minutes. I have chosen an outfit – pale blue with a loose blouse and a skirt slit at the side – and only really need to put it on to be ready. I have also picked out a pair of heels to wear, which is something I rarely do, even at my petite 5'4" – after all, nursing has no place for high heels. I persuade her to come in and scrub my back for me – a little luxury for me I have enjoyed since I was a young girl – then go and dress, apply a very little make up and perfume, and wait for Simon to arrive. I almost laugh out loud at Mama, who is prowling between the kitchen, living room and front door, looking at the clock and fretting.

Simon is on time and has brought flowers for Mama and a bottle of wine for us. I introduce him to Mama, and he greets her by kissing her on the cheek. Mama does not even try to disguise her sizing him up, looking him up and down.

"You're getting taller", she says to me with a smile, and I stifle a laugh. This is a little in joke – she rarely criticised Andrei to me but when she did, his short stature was always a feature. Simon looks back and forth between us for a moment, a little puzzled, and I hold a hand up and tell him that Mama had just said that he was very tall, and I leave it at that. Mama has been holding my upper arm in both hands since the moment I opened the door, leaving me to take her flowers, but with one more appraising look she squeezes my arm, pats me on the shoulder and kisses me on the cheek, before taking the flowers and disappearing almost magically into her room without another word.

Mama has made sarmale and mici for dinner for us, and Simon and I eat together across my dining table and drink his wine. He certainly seems to enjoy the food, and when he asks, I have to be honest and tell him it is all Mama's cooking. Mama leaves the two of us alone for the evening – I listen out for her but don't even hear any movement, and then we sit on my couch – or rather Simon sits on the couch, and I sit on him – and cuddle, and talk and kiss. I want very much to take him to bed with me but when it gets late, he gets up to leave, tells me what a lovely evening he has had and asks me to tell Mama that it was a pleasure to meet her and that she made a lovely meal.

Once the door closes behind him, Mama reappears just as magically as when she disappeared in the first place.

"He's handsome," she says, "is he a good man?"

"He is – and he said to tell you the dinner was excellent"

"And he is a smart man", she adds.

"How would you know, you spent no time talking to him? I brought him here so you two could meet!"

"Of course he is a smart man – firstly, he knows to bring flowers to your Mother and to praise her cooking, second he is in love with you."

I look at her sceptically.

"You have the eyes, but you don't see, do you? You should see the way he looks at you, my love. There is a man who would give you his heart and his soul, if you asked him to."

I remain sceptical that she can have reached this conclusion bearing in mind their limited interaction and say so. Mama puts her arm around me which I initially take as an expression of affection and go to hug her back, but instead she begins guiding me to the kitchen.

"Dishes" she says. With a smile on my lips as I think about what Mama has said, and I do as I am told, leaving the heels by the front door.

Ella

The transition of Anna moving out and Grazyna – well, Grace now – moving in goes smoothly, but then Anna had so little stuff that she wanted to take with her, and Grace had so little stuff at all that that kind of makes sense. Grace is very different to how I remember her – she seems, I don't know, more human almost. She is warmer to me than I remember, uncomfortably so sometimes, but she is still my sister and I love her so when she wants to cuddle up to me on the couch and watch my TV with me, I let her. When she has terrible rows with her husband on the phone and cries in my lap for what seems like hours afterwards, I say all the right things and stroke her annoyingly perfect hair while she makes blorting noises and snots into a tissue. When Mama calls and there is more crying and she comes to me for a hug, I hold her and tell her that it's all OK and that Mama loves her very much.

Fortunately, for both of us, Grace's husband does not call again after the first month or so, which bearing in mind what Grace has told me between blorts and snots is not surprising. Mama calls once or twice a week, and as time moves on it becomes a joint call with Grace passing me the phone after a little while. Grace now has these wide ranging and what sound like an adventurous retelling of her week with Mama, whilst mine are stilted and more rooted in reality – to listen to Grace, a trip to the supermarket was a quest into foreign lands beset by challenges and diversions supported only by wits and a trusty sidekick (me) and a gallant hero who brought his mighty green and blue steed to our rescue and takes about an hour to retell. To listen to me, we went to Tesco on the bus.

I am incredibly grateful, though, for the company again. My little house has come alive – where I would lay in bed listening to emptiness now I hear Grace getting up to use the bathroom or get a drink of water. Grace and I go to the local pubs and introduce to her my favourite one, the one that serves Tyskie. We sometimes see Anna at the house and at the pub, and Anna and Grace form quite a bond – where Anna used to pick out men for me, now Anna and Grace pick out men for each other – although Anna assures us that she and Alan are very much together – and I am a spectator to their game and their occasional mock outrage. With a new playmate Anna seems much less interested in my love life which is no bad thing.

However, just because Grace was living with me now did not make my worries about money go away. When she came here, she came with some money and for a while had access to, presumably, her husband's accounts, but that stopped at about the same time the phone calls did. Anna was true to her word and continued to pay her portion of the rent, but I knew that I could not rely on that forever – so when a job for senior care worker came up at the local hospital, I applied. I had some good experience, had done my level two and level three qualifications and, honestly, needed the money. As nice as it was to have Grace at the pub with us – or as nice at it was to eat food, buy clothes or go on the bus for that matter – Grace was not contributing much.

I meet the manager at my interview, a tall man called Mr Holcroft – he has the kind of English accent that I had expected that all English people have, only to be sorely disappointed once I was actually here, and I like the sound of it. He is showing me around the ward – it looks much like the place I am planning to leave, that is, full of old people, only some of these ones look older than time itself, presumably through illness. There are a few staff around too, and Mr Holcroft introduces me. If I am any judge, I would say that the interview has gone well – it would be a harsh person who would introduce me to a lot of people that I will never meet again – so I am not surprised when a job offer lands on the doormat about a week later which I ring up and accept.

With my induction out of the way I set to getting to work, and I learn that my first impression of the ward is pretty accurate – it is a lot like the last place, with cleaning and washing and dressing and feeding – but it does have some added elements I enjoy as I learn about observations and interpreting them, knowing what to report and what not to. Also, I am a little surprised to learn that there are 'factions' here, again, unlike the care home. There we got on and did what was needed, working as a team; here there is one faction in particular who seem to be determined to avoid work at all costs. I do all I can not to align myself with them, thank you, but find that instead they come to me to hand off their tasks to me to do – even some of the staff that are technically junior to me will pass on their duties so that they can do something else that is never clearly defined.

I am a little surprised and concerned when Mr Holcroft calls me to his office one day and tells me that I am not working effectively.

"I am working as hard as I can!" I exclaim, not too confrontationally as he is the boss after all, but I am taken aback.

"Yes, I have seen you," he says, "taking on things from other people and working hard to complete them – but you are a senior and need to manage the workload amongst the staff, not take it all on yourself. Karen for example, needs direction and supervision and is junior to you, which does not mean you just doing her work for her – if she says she can't do something, teach her so that she can in future. You're a smart girl and a hard worker, but I need you to do more of the former and less of the latter. Work smarter, not harder!" he adds, and looks pleased with himself.

I am not too happy about being called a girl, but otherwise I can see his point.

The next few weeks I take on what the boss has said and start directing back the work that seems to head my way and I can see that this is not well received by the Karens on the ward but that this gets me a lot of support from a lot of the rest of the staff, especially one of the nurses called Alina. She tells me to ignore the ones that don't want to work and pretty much repeats what Mr Holcroft said word for word about providing direction and supervision, which is interesting; her and Mr Holcroft – or Simon as she tells me his name is – along with a couple of other staff, seem to be in a faction all of their own. Whether it says it on the staff rota or not, she is definitely his lieutenant and I wonder whether he shares all of his conversations at work with her.

Alina has a way of studying you whilst you work, whilst completing her own work with a fastidiousness and alacrity that I haven't seen in other people – I learn to respect her and to respect her judgement, and I find that the more I am seen working with her and with her attitude, the less likely I am to have any problems with any Karens. In fact, Karen leaves to be replaced by a Katy and the workers-against-work faction, before long, seems to consist only of a girl called Vicky who makes no secret that she is looking for another job too.

Overall, I am pleased that I made the move to this new job – the better money helps, as does the fact that Grace found herself a job waitressing in a restaurant where her charm – and probably her good looks too – earn her a lot of tips and one or two phone numbers as well, although she doesn't take up any of the offers as far as I know. As well as the money I am learning a lot, and if there is one thing I know about myself it is that I like to learn things. Yes, there is the clinical aspects that sometimes fascinate me, and I find myself reading textbooks for pleasure so that I can share my new knowledge at work, but it is also understanding the dynamics of working in this place, the undercurrent of small battles and ground won and lost, and I gain respect for Mr Holcroft – Simon – too, for riding this current like a surfer.

It is a shock, then, when seemingly without cause, he announces that he is leaving.

Alina

It is a shock when he tells me that he has told the staff that he is going to leave work, but after a little explanation I understand why he has. He tells me that he is already in breach "of about a thousand" HR rules for being in a relationship with me in the first place. He tells me that he is in love with me and that he wants to take things more seriously, which means going public, which – if he remains my boss – means a lot of trouble for him at work.

The thing is that I know that he likes his work, that he likes making what he sees as his ward a success, likes seeing people well looked after and likes to see happy staff. Since Karen left the only ugly wart on an otherwise happy landscape is Vicky, who despite her efforts just can't seem to get another job. I asked Simon about what he thought the problem was and he would only cryptically reply that her problem was that he wouldn't lie about her.

It troubles me greatly that he will have to give up his job for us, but even more than that it troubles me that he might be this committed to us. I realise that I am not making myself very clear so I will try to explain as best as I can.

The thing is I am not certain that I am in love with him – yes, I enjoy seeing him, I enjoy making love with him (we stopped calling it sex some time ago, and it has changed and for the better). I like going out with him or staying in with him, I like talking to him and just being around him, I do love him, but I can only think that being in love with him would mean giving myself away to him and I can't do that – not now and not ever again. I feel things for him, and when I am with him, and when I am away from him, but is that all that love is? A feeling in the stomach? I can live without stomach feelings.

I try explaining this to him as a reason why leaving work is such a bad idea. It does not go well.

"What do you mean?", he asks.

"Your career is important to you, obviously…" I begin but am cut off.

"Fuck that!" he cries – and I can see what look like tears in his eyes, "What do mean you can never be in love with me? What the fuck is wrong with being in love with me? I tell you that I am in love with you and your response is to, broadly, tell me I am barking up the wrong tree? What the fuck is wrong with you?"

I don't fully understand what he has just said about trees, say so, and again, I try to embark on an explanation, but it seems clear that I cannot make myself understood, or if not that, that he is in no position to listen. In my head I can hear the domestic violence social worker telling me not to get into a relationship – good or bad – and I have for weeks been trying to work out how I will introduce Simon to Christiana, or even if I want to, to bring a man into her life that she has no choice over. And what about if we want to live together, how will that work? Sharing myself between my daughter and a man, living under the same roof.

I don't think that he is angry, but he is giving a very good impression of it – his face is red, his voice is raised, and I am seeing him shaking, but I don't feel threatened; if I were to judge, he looks like the men I have nursed after who, after a lifetime of being brave and manly, have no more to look forward to except days or weeks of unremitting pain. I hate myself for being so clinical at a time like this, and as if to confirm my diagnosis the tears that he has threatened do indeed come and now it is my turn to feel a pain in my heart that I am causing him to feel this way.

I try again.

"I know you are a good man, and yes, you are handsome and kind to me, but being in love means I cannot be myself any more, that I will belong to you and I cannot let that happen to me and Christiana." I know that I believe every word and I try to give them the solemnity that they deserve.

He looks incredulous – he even looks around the room as if my words have come from somewhere else, from some source he can't identify. When he turns back to me, he is no less pained "Is that what you think love means? That you have to lose all sense of yourself? That's fucking insane!"

I am not insane. Even in that moment I am certain that I am doing the sanest thing I can think to do which is to not get involved too deeply and pull away before it is too late to change anything, before I end up trapped again with someone who now only wants me for what I provide for them; a trophy, an income, a hole to fuck. I walk over to from where I am standing by the kitchen to sit next to where he has collapsed onto his sofa and rest my hand on his arm. He doesn't move.

"You are a good man", I repeat, "you will find someone else to be in love with, it just can't be me, do you understand? How about that new girl, Ella? She's pretty." And I can see that I have said completely the wrong thing from his expression, and I can see that he thinks I must be cold and heartless, but if he could only see inside me, he would see my pain – I don't want to push this man away, but I must. I cannot allow him to fall in love with me because I know how hard I will fall in love with him, too.

I don't know where the suggestion of Ella came from, but she is a good person and yes, she is pretty and smart too and I know Simon could make her happy, but I reflect briefly that this was an ill-advised moment to bring her up. I sit there for a while, no words being exchanged, just my hand resting on his arm as his tears run down his face. I want to kiss them away and tell him that it is all OK and I was wrong but I can't – this is not a fairy-tale either and real life has stripped me of my fantasies. To love, to live, means to suffer, not to be rescued, not to be set free, but to be confined. I will not be confined, no matter how pleasant the prison or how handsome the jailer.

After a while I get up to leave.

"I better go"

"Stay"

"I can't, I have to get home," this is true, "and what more is there to say or do?" I pick up my coat which had been slung over the back of a chair.

I am at the door and leave my key – no, I leave the spare key – on the table.

"I will never stop loving you, Alina," he says after me, "I will always love you."

I hold back my own tears as I close the door after me. It's cold out tonight, and I shiver in my coat, pushing my hands deep into my pockets. I can see my own breath as I sigh into the night and whisper, "Si eu te iubesc" – so it looks like the words made real dissolve in right front of my blurry eyes.

Dee

He rings me in a mess. He has clearly had a bad break up that he is not handling well, and he asks if he can see me.

I tell him no. Not that I am too busy, not that I have an excuse, just no.

I have spent too much time since that meeting in London thinking about Simon and, yes, missing him and the sex we would have and picking up my phone to call or text in the hope of a reply or that we will pick up from where we were again, but it was Becca who told me what I needed to hear – Simon had made his choice and moved on, and so I needed to as well, and either decide that my future was with Ben or that it wasn't and leave Ben for good.

I decided that Ben was my future.

I had come back from that meeting tearful, fuming and frustrated and walked straight into Becca as soon as I returned – she had come bounding over, looking eager to hear about everything but took one look at my face and realised that this was not going to be one of those conversations. We didn't have time then to discuss but quickly made plans to meet up at hers after work that night, although she did insist taking me down to radiology to get an x-ray done of my hand – nothing broken, fortunately.

I told her everything there was to tell – which amounted to very little, really, and we spent most of the time drinking ourselves stupid and declaring that all men are cunts and Simon in particular. I don't know whose idea it was but we ended up in her bed and had sex – well, more like a drunken fumble really – but I remember she came and I came and then waking up groggy and naked the next morning with her laying on me dribbling on my right tit and her hand between my thighs. I extricated myself, cleaned up in her bathroom and by the time I was back she was awake.

"Oof" she said, "some night", rubbing her head with one hand and, I suspect, her pussy under the duvet with the other. With her smeared make up it looked like she had been punched in both eyes and I told her. "I feel like I have too", she said, flashing a smile and looking up. "MMhmmm, told you, cracking bod" she added, making no effort to hide looking me up and down. I know I blushed from head to foot as I scurried around looking for where my clothes were – somehow, I could only find one sock, my vest was nowhere to be seen and my knickers were torn at the hip. Some night indeed.

Since I made my walk of shame home that morning neither Becca nor I have spoken of it again, nor, despite numerous nights of copious alcohol, has it happened again, and I am a little relieved. I think we have both put it down to a one-off in extenuating circumstances.

It was a few days after that night that Becca sat me down in the staff canteen and laid it all out for me – I could not continue running around the place having my cake and eating it, or as she put it "having my cake and being eaten out". I had to make a choice about what it was that I wanted; did I want stability and security, or did I want to carry on along this path of "fucking around". Looking back, I wonder if that was her way of asking if I wanted to be with her, but I am doubtful – neither before or since has she given any indication that she might be lesbian and I am certainly not, although some days I do wish I could remember more of that night, but on others I am grateful that it is all a bit of a haze that seems less real as time moves on.

Like I said, I decided then and there that Ben was my future and said so – Becca nodded knowingly, told me I was making a good choice, and then got on with general office gossip and demolishing a large cheeseburger and chips – she knows exactly what I feel about eating meat and has told me many times that she doesn't care and if it bothers me, I should sit somewhere else. It doesn't bother me enough to do that, so I usually just make a grimacing face at her and leave it at that. She pinches my bum as we walk back to the lab and jogs away giggling.

Ben seemed to appreciate that I was throwing myself into our marriage with renewed vigour. I went to watch rally driving with him, one of his passions, even though it was, as I suspected it would be, cold and wet and quite a long period of boredom punctuated by noise and terror that is over in the blink of an eye as a car flies past. I asked him to come and watch a play at the Globe with me, and he did, and had the good grace not to grumble about it afterwards. We have more sex now, although we have no toys (mine I discreetly disposed of) and it is not as fulfilling for me as it was with Simon, but the longer time goes on the less I think about him and the sex and everything else and the more I believe that this life with Ben is the life that I want.

So, when Simon rings me, of course I say no to him. He has no place in this life that I have carved out for myself, a life which, to be frank, he helped to carve out for me. Also, I am not drawn to the mess of a man I hear on the phone – stuttering and uncertain, adrift almost. The Simon I know is determined and strong and dominant, not this lost child missing his latest favourite toy. I don't even understand why he is so cut up about it – he has always been, as far as I am aware, an unreliable person to think of as a partner/boyfriend/husband. He couldn't stick at marriage, he couldn't stick at us, he hasn't stuck at his latest conquest. Fuck him. Or rather more accurately, don't fuck him.

I am probably quite harsh with him and as far as I am concerned, he deserves it. We end the call cordially but no more than that – I hover over the 'block caller' button on my phone but decide against it – I am not sure why I don't press it. I tell Becca that he has called – and all about the call except the block caller decision – and I ask her if I did the right thing. She tells me that of course I did and down that path lays madness and heartbreak.

She is right of course – after all, if it weren't for Simon's unreliability a very nice pair of lacy knickers wouldn't have gotten torn and a vest wouldn't have been lost in what she rightly describes as a fit of madness.

Ella

Something is happening and I am not sure what it is. After the manager tells us that he is leaving I see someone on the ward that I don't recognise, but she is wearing a trouser suit and has a hospital ID badge. I see her ask at reception, see Alina being pointed out, then watch her go over to Alina and introduce herself. Seconds later she is leading Alina over to the manager's office.

Less than five minutes pass before I see Alina leave, looking disturbed – or at least as disturbed as I have ever seen her, which is admittedly has not been a lot. A minute or so after that and the new lady leaves, straightening her jacket unconsciously, and less than a minute after that I see Mr Holcroft striding from the ward, his suit jacket over his arm and bag in hand. He doesn't come back for the rest of the day.

The next time I see her a day or so later I want to ask Alina what is going on, but she definitely has a 'don't you dare talk to me' face on and seems to be going out of her way not to talk to anyone. Mr Holcroft is in but has been hidden away in his office all day until he leaves, again somewhat abruptly, halfway through the afternoon. I watch Alina watching him go with a momentary sadness in her eyes. She catches me watching her watching him, and instead of the expected telling off, she nods towards the staff room. I get the hint, finish the bed change I was half through, and head there discreetly. She closes the patient notes folder she had been writing in, tucks it under her arm and follows me.

"What's this about," I ask, "have I done something wrong?"

"No, no, not at all," she says taking me gently by the upper arm, "I just wanted to talk to you, that's all."

I relax a little, but not much.

"As you know Simon, Mr Holcroft, is leaving and – well, there's no other way to say it but he will be going sooner than any of us expected. They want him to go back downstairs to run the Emergency department. He leaves the end of this week."

I feel, and clearly look a bit shocked at this. I didn't think that that was how things work around here. Alina presses on. "Well, Matron Wilshire wants me to take over here, that was her I think you saw the other day? Well, it looks like Mr Holcroft has been saying good things about me and she has listened, so she is putting me in charge – at least, temporarily."

"Oh wow, congratulations!" I say, "But I don't understand what that has to do with me or why you are telling me?"

"That's the thing – he has been saying good things about you too, and I have been watching how you work and how you are around the other staff. I know you have not been here that long, but once I take over, I would like you to consider being a team leader."

I have to sit down for a minute. I didn't even know that anyone was paying attention to me, let alone talking about me behind closed doors. I have a brief moment of paranoia before realising that this is a good thing.

"It will come with a little bit of a salary bump, but will mean additional responsibilities too," continues Alina, "but both Si.. – I mean, Mr Holcroft – and I think you're right for the job."

"Will I need an interview or anything?" I ask.

"The job is yours if you want," she replies, "just let me know as soon as you can."

I tell her I'll take a day or two to think about, knowing that I have already accepted it in my head. Mr Holcroft is in the next day and put my head tentatively round his door as I tap gently, the moment I am able between patients.

"Ella, come in!" he says warmly.

"I've spoken to Alina," I blurt out with no thought of how I was going to say this, "and I wanted to say thank you."

"What for?"

"For the promotion opportunity...?" I say, thinking for a moment I must have misunderstood what was going on.

"Ah, so she is offering you team leader, is she?" he smiles back at me, "that's good, you're an excellent choice."

"You didn't know?"

"No, but I am not surprised. I have been saying for some time how hard you work and how you have come along really well since starting here. I am very pleased for you, I think you'll do great." He is still smiling at me, and I believe that he is genuinely pleased for me.

"Well, all the same I wanted to say thank you, Mr Holcroft."

"Nothing to thank me for, Ella, it was all you. Oh, and it's just plain Simon – I'm not the boss anymore."

I get up to leave and as I do, half turn and say "Well, thank you anyway Mr..... I mean, S-s-simon." I stumble over the word, and I don't know why but I feel embarrassed. I can feel myself flush. I scurry out.

True enough, by the following week Simon is gone and Alina is in charge. Nearly everyone seems happy with the new boss and misses the old boss, except for Vicky who looks infuriated. When Alina announces me as the new team leader Vicky's tiny eyes seem to ignite into an undisguised hatred. I pretend not to notice.

Alina closes with letting us all know that there will be a get together at the end of the week to say goodbye to Mr Holcroft and hopes everyone will attend, and the number of nods and approving noises makes me think it will be well attended, and sure enough it is – it looks like everyone not on duty joins the party (except Vicky) and I take up my usual position at parties of trying to melt into the wall and indulge in some people watching, so I see that there is still some tension between Alina and Simon, who seem to be going to great lengths to avoid each other. Alina makes a beeline for me later, though, a drink in each hand offering me one, and tells me that she hopes that she and I will be good friends, and that, just between me and her, she is a lot like me, someone you're more likely to find at the edge of a party than the centre of it. We drink our drinks, something appley and strong and she tells me something of her life and I tell her something of mine – I think the drink makes me think of home home so she even gets to hear a bit about the orchards.

She tells me a little about Simon, too, and tells me with a sadness in her eyes that he is a good man and that she will miss him. She seems a little drunk and I think that we wouldn't be having this conversation if both of us were completely sober. I can see that there is, or at least was, a closeness between these two, and that as much as she is trying to hide her emotions, they are leaking through eyes. I tell her that I think he is too, and that seems to cheer her up. She asks apropos of nothing whether I have a boyfriend, and when I say that I haven't, says that she thinks Simon and I would be a good match. "You're tall like him", she says, waving a hand to indicate height and with almost a finality to the point she is making. I think it is the apple liquor that is making her talk nonsense, although I see another flash of sadness cross her face, before she is smiling brightly, if a little forcedly. I make a show of appraising him from across the room – I have done this enough times with Anna to make a good show of it – put my head on the side and purse my lips as though thinking.

"Hmmm, maybe…" I say and then laugh – this drink is strong! – and I am happy to see Alina laughing along with me.

Alina

I am late.

Oh, fuck.

Dee

I call him about three months later, realising that it wasn't him that had abandoned me, I had abandoned him when I had told him that I wasn't going to leave Ben for him. I don't tell Becca that I plan to do this – to be honest, we have not even raised the subject of Simon since he called last time and Becca reassured me that I was doing the right thing so, as calling him now feels a little like betraying her I have, sensibly I think, not said a word about it.

He seems genuinely pleased to hear from me and seems to be a lot happier and more together, much more like the Simon I know. He tells me he has moved on in his job as well as his love life and asks me how things are with Ben. I don't want to tell him about Ben, that has always been how things are, and I think he senses the hesitation in my voice.

"Look, whatever else we are I think we can agree that we are friends, right?"

I think I can agree to that.

"So I am just asking how you are which means asking about Ben too..."

I think I can see his point.

"...but if it is making you uncomfortable you don't need to tell me anything..."

It is making me uncomfortable and I don't want to tell him anything, or at least tell him anything about Ben.

"...but I do want you to know that I will always be here if I can help in any way..."

Which is where exactly, these days?

"...because whatever else we'll always be close, don't you think?"

I do think. And then he tells me that he is back in the Emergency department, a place I know he loved, seeing someone and that it is going pretty well – I don't get any more detail than that. I tell him that Ben and I are planning to tour Europe in a few months' time and Simon seems genuinely excited for me at the prospect. After I hang up, I realise that I am pleased that he sounds happier and much more like himself and I am glad that I called, but it is clear from the call that we have both moved on in our lives. I promise to make sure that we meet up for coffee before I leave, although if I am honest, I am not sure that I will keep that promise – too much time has passed, too much water under the bridge. I reflect that whilst we have each moved on, the 'us' that we were has moved on too – his assertion that we will always be close and he will always do what he can for me if I need him rings true, I know we have built a connection that not everyone will have or understand, and that it has changed in ways probably neither of us suspected when we first embarked on it.

I don't tell Becca that I have spoken to Simon afterwards either, instead I feel an urge to speak to Sarah. We have stayed in touch, even when she moved back to the West Indies a while ago, and we talk on text messaging every couple of weeks or so. I text her and we arrange to have a proper conversation in a day or two once we work out the time differences.

She is pleased to hear from me, we talk about this and that, about the tour of Europe coming up for Ben and me, but there must be some catch in my voice that lets her see right through me, just like she always could. Even without being able to see my face she still knows when I am not saying something, and I can imagine her making the Pirate Face at the other end of the phone.

"What did you really want, Denise?" She is incredibly good at coming to the point.

I tell her everything – and I mean everything – and it pours out of me like water through a broken dam. She listens to me apologise for lying to her, back when we lived together, all the time we worked together and for keeping this part of my life away from her this whole time. I even cry a little as I say sorry to her time and time again for lying to her. It is like I am seeking her disapproval and I want to hear her tell me what an idiot I have been so that I can get over this man that made my head spin for a while.

Fortunately, she is happy to provide the disapproval I seek.

"Girl, you're a damn fool. You better tell me right now that you're not seeing that man again. I knew, I *knew* that you were telling tales to me, girl, and I knew the trouble you would get yourself into. That husband of yours deserves better, my girl, he deserves better! He has done nothing but take care of you since the day you two met and this is how you have repaid him all these years."

She is so angry with me that the West Indian accent is getting so strong I struggle to understand all the words that spill out.

"You tell me right now, girl, you tell me you ain't seeing that man again. Then you march straight back home and you tell that husband of yours what a good man he is to you, how glad you are you married him and you make him feel like a king for once. A king! You hearing me?"

I assure her I am.

"You stay away from that man – he is no good for you, no damn good at all. You love him?"

I stammer and mutter that I am not sure.

"Then you're more of a fool that I thought! You mark well, girly, he ain't no kind of man to love, your Benny, he's a man you can love."

She is right, of course – there is no point in being in love with someone who you can't be with, and I am long past the time when I should have listened to myself, but instead, just like so many times in the past, it has had to be Sarah to tell me what I already knew.

She has a few choice words to say about Becca too, and I realise that she is right about this as well – Becca encouraged me because she had nothing to lose, it wasn't her that was married to Ben, it wasn't her that was sneaking around in random hotels, it wasn't her that was taking the risks, she had no skin in the game. Sarah tells me that Becca is a 'poison' which I say is a little harsh, but I do so pretty meekly having been brow beaten so thoroughly. At some level I understand that the whole reason I was drawn to Becca in the first place, and consequently drifted away from Sarah, was because she is not Sarah and Sarah would have told me from the outset what a fool I was being, have been outraged with what I was getting up to, and Becca would not.

I apologise to Sarah with this in mind. She tells me I should be apologising to Ben.

The call ends with me promising to call her more often, because it is clear to Sarah that without her around I go off the rails – I resist the temptation to say that even when she was around I was still seeing Simon – and with her making me promise three times over that I will not be seeing or getting in touch with Simon again, and I find that I do mean it.

I take some flowers home for Ben feeling exhausted and a little broken – I don't know what else to do – and he is surprised to say the least. I tell him that he is special and that I am proud of him and that I am sorry. Naturally, he asks me what for and I flannel a bit and say it is for not always valuing him enough or in the way that I should and for not telling him often enough how lucky I am to have him in my life. I cry a little and he cuddles me and then we have Chinese takeout cuddled up on the sofa with some nature programme on and I understand that for everything Ben isn't, he is safe, he is steady, and he will never leave me, and I realise that that is something that I do love him for. He doesn't push me to talk, he just holds me and comments on the elephants and offers me a cup of tea roughly fifteen times an hour until we go to bed. And then, for the first time in a long time, I curl myself around him, pull his arms around me, and lay there being held – and I sleep and I don't dream at all.

Ella

We ran into each other, practically, whilst I was on my way down to the canteen for break. I almost walked straight into him in the corridor – I habitually walk with my eyes to the ground anyway and was idly browsing my mobile at the time as well. He asked me how it was going, and did I like being team leader and I told him that it was going well and that yes, being team leader was good – and it was too. I felt like I had been growing into the role over the last couple of months and despite my initial trepidation I was glad I had taken on the job.

He asks me about the unit and when I tell him that the hospital left Alina in charge, he tells me that he already knows and asks me to wish her well for him. I promise I will do. He is about to walk on and past when I stop to ask him if he would like to come for a drink with me some time.

Of course, it wasn't as straight forward as me actually using the words, "would you like to come for a drink with me" and I felt like I was standing there with a bright red face for at least an hour as I ummed and ahhed and hesitated. I say something about Grace and me going to the pub, sometimes with Anna and sometimes without, and that they serve Tyskie which I am very pleased about, obviously aware that he has no idea who either of the people are that I am talking about and probably no idea about Polish beer either.

He looks a cross between confused and amused until I get to the "we'll be there, err, Thursday night, you know, ummm, if you wanted to, you know The Oaks, if you wanted to come down?" when it finally seems to make sense to him, he smiles warmly and tells me he will see us there, but he's got to go right now.

He sets off again and I start heading back towards the ward – which means walking in the same direction as him – before remembering I still have to get something to eat, so I sort of stop, look both ways along the corridor, stammer some sort of mumbled apology (what for and who to I don't know) and head back toward the canteen.

I make the decision there and then that I am not going to tell either Grace or Anna about this because they will both make a big deal about it and that is the last thing I want, but it is a bit more challenging when Thursday comes and neither of them want to go to the pub tonight – Anna wants to go home to Alan, and Grace doesn't want to have to get dressed. Either one of them will do, but I complain at them both for long enough that they both agree to go, and I hustle Grace along and text Anna every few minutes to make sure she is coming. Grace does seem to be livelier once I have got her to change out of her pyjamas – which she has been in all day if I am any judge – and Anna gets fed up with my texting her and stops responding after a final

    FFS ILL BE THERE

and I know I have annoyed her because the punctuation is missing and there's no x at the end.

We get there about 8, usual time for us but I begin to worry that he has been and gone again having not found me here earlier.

The Oaks is quite an old pub. We find some nice seats, kind of like two-seater benches, with high backs and a table between them, and I get us three pints whilst Anna and Grace manoeuvre themselves down one side of the table. The barman recognises us so when I say three pints, he doesn't even ask me what of, and heads straight for the Tyskie.

The pub has two sets of double doors at the front, one set external in white chipped old paint, one internal of worn bare wood, and all four doors creak when they are opened. Usually, this forms a sort of background to the general hubbub, but tonight I am acutely aware of the doors being used. I also realise that I can tell whether someone is entering or leaving by the order, pitch and tone of the squeaks. Not exactly a useful talent in any other circumstances, but feeling as on edge as I am, every time there is an entering person (low pitch and drawn-out squeak, followed by a higher pitch two stage cascading then descending creak if you're interested), I look round from our table. After about a half an hour of this, it has not escaped the attention of either Anna or Grace.

"What's the matter with you?" asks Grace, taking a deep drink from her glass, "You look like one of those things, you know the furry... they bob up and down, you know... in the desert..."

"Meerkats!" blurts out Anna, "That's what you look like!"

"Meerkats! Exactly! What's the matter anyway? Bobbing your head up and down like a meerkat. Your head looks like it is on a swivel."

I open my mouth to say something when the door creaks as someone enters and I automatically look round.

"There you go again!", exclaims Grace, pointing her glass at first me, then the door.

Anna elbows her meaningfully, I presume trying to look like the detective that has finally cracked the case, drawing out the sentence. "She is waiting for someone."

"Ow!! Who?"

"Well, look at her, she has dressed up the occasion – I did wonder why she was finally wearing that top I bought her... last Christmas, wasn't it?"

"No, you bought me that top and I told you it was too tight for me, remember? I said you should take it back and get me a gift card, but I see it has been repurposed."

"Sorry, I underestimated the size of your tits" Anna says, turning her head slightly and briefly to cast a withering look at Grace's chest, "an easy mistake to make. Hmm, look at her face."

And they sit there, both with their arms folded, critically examining me like they are David Attenboroughs and I am a brand new species or something.

"Tense, agitated…"

"Flushed too, and ooo look it's getting worse!"

I am beginning to hate them both and glower at them from my side of the table.

"She's your sister, have you ever seen her looking like that?"

"Only when she's sick…"

"She's not sick, that wouldn't make her jumpy".

"What then?"

Anna slaps her hand down on the table and looks more pleased with herself than anyone has any right to be.

"It's a man!" she hoots, "She's invited a man! Haven't you?"

"My God you're right, it's a man isn't it!"

"She's almost purple now…Tell me this, are you wearing matching underwear?"

I ignore the question, fume and hiss "Shut. Up."

"It IS a man! BARKEEP?" Anna practically stands in her seat so that she can wave energetically waving her glass in the direction of the bar, spilling beer over the back of the seat. "DRINKS! WE'RE CELEBRATING!"

"Shut UP!"

They both fall about, laughing until they both look like they're gasping for breath.

By this point my head is so low over my drink, and feels so hot, I half expect my beer to boil away. They both embark on an interrogation, but between them they don't leave me a space to speak, filling in the blanks themselves, so I hear that it must be someone from work (true) because I never go out (untrue), someone they don't know (true) because otherwise they would already know about it (also true, I suppose), he's got to be a bit desperate (harsh), especially once he sees my underpants drawer (Anna), although I "look like" have made a bit of an effort (Grace), I probably have put on matching underwear (Anna), am not wearing black for a change (Anna) and overall I don't look too bad (both of them). Anna tells me to show her my bra strap so that she can tell what set I have got on and that it "better not" (sternly wagging a finger at me) "be grey".

This is beginning to feel like a terrible mistake, and Simon chooses that moment to walk in whilst Anna and Grace are in fits of hysterics. Of course, by this time Anna and Grace are so alert to anyone coming in the door, and in any case have a better view than I do, that they see him before I do – and because I am still hoping the table and bench will open up and swallow me whole.

"Is that him?" says Grace, turning to me. Anna has jumped up on her seat again and is still looking, very obviously sizing him up. Eventually she stops kneeling on the seat to look over the back of my bench seat and turns back to me.

"Is that him? Not bad..." she finishes before I have a chance to answer. God only knows what we must look like to Simon, with two of us bobbing up and down over the back of the bench, smiling like idiots and laughing like drains.

I wave nervously to Simon, and he waves back and starts heading towards our table. Grace and Anna share a look first with each other, then with me that could not have been more coordinated if it had been rehearsed. Simon reaches the end of the table, leans over it, and kisses me on the cheek as he says Hi. I introduce him to Anna and Grace, and he kisses them on a proffered cheek each as well, which seems to go down well with them. They are both now smiling beatifically as though they are both angels brought to earth, which they most certainly are not.

He offers to buy a round and we all accept, then when he comes back to the table, he sits next to me.

The evening goes very well, all things considered – he makes me feel comfortable and chats easily to Anna and Grace and seems really interested in what they both do. He listens patiently and involves me in the conversation, which is difficult at first as I am still feeling unsettled, not least of which thanks to them both just before he came in, but as I feel myself calm down – and possibly as we have another couple of drinks – we settle down. We talk about all sorts of things, and he often knows something of the topic, but where he doesn't, he asks intelligent and probing questions. He gives every impression of being interested in the answers, too. He asks about where Grace and I grew up, which is not somewhere I particularly want to talk about, but Grace makes it sound like a magical land where the sun always shone and the trees where ladened with fruit practically all year round and the apples were better than any apples in the history of the world. I am exaggerating, but only a little because she does not describe it the way I remember it. He doesn't seem to notice or comment that Anna and me always buy Grace's round, and he even starts doing it too.

For all the discomfort and anxiety I felt tonight, it was a good night. It is getting late when the three of us get up to leave, but as I do so he stops me and asks if he can have my number, and I give it to him. He immediately texts me so that I have his too.

There is another round of kisses on the cheek as the three of us set off back home – it is so late now I suspect Anna will crash at mine – and we start the walk back.

I am barely two minutes down the street when my phone beeps again:

> Hi Ella – you've forgotten something.

I start checking my pockets as I text back:

> What is it? Can you drop it off at work for me?

> Not really – you better come back for a minute.

"You two go ahead," I say, starting back for the pub, "I've left something at the pub, I'll catch you up."

They both shrug and carry on walking.

As I come up the slight hill, I can see him standing outside the pub waiting patiently for me.

"What have I forgotten?" I ask.

"This" he says, as he gently holds my face in both hands and kisses me gently on the lips. The kiss seems both to last for ages and not nearly long enough, but I do have time to bring my arms up and around his neck and reciprocate.

Then he pulls away, takes both my hands in his and away from his neck, smiles and says "Goodnight", enigmatically looking over my shoulder and smiling before turning and heading away. He doesn't look back. I turn to head down the hill again to see Anna and Grace stood arm in arm a little way away, grinning like Cheshire Cats. I can't help but smile too.

Alina

I can't possibly be pregnant. I can't. I mean, I know it is biologically possible, but I can't, not now. I mean, likely not ever, but really not now.

It's something else, it has to be something else – I haven't been eating well, I know that it's been stressful with the new job, I can't be pregnant. Usually as regular as clockwork, two days becomes four, four becomes a week, a week becomes a month and by then, even though I am having nausea most mornings (could be stress of the job, right? Right???) it is not until I am sat on my toilet at home looking at two lines that it begins to sink in as a potential reality. Even then, I go out and buy another three kits, one after the other, drinking as much water as I can stomach, so I can pee on a stick and see two lines again.

I am sitting on my toilet, surrounded by cardboard and plastic packaging and dual lines, and I start to cry – no, that's not true, I sob. For the briefest of moments, I consider getting an abortion, then immediately hate myself for having that thought. There is no way I would or could ever terminate a child, and that makes me think of the child that is already growing inside me and I look down and stroke my belly with tears in my eyes and dripping off my chin.

I don't know how long I sit there but I hear the front door bang to wake me from my reverie. Christiana is home from school. What do I tell her? Nothing, I tell her nothing, comes the answer. I clear up the rubbish that is all around me, put it all in the little bin in the bathroom, take the bag out and tie it in a knot. As I come out of the bathroom Christiana is throwing her school bag down on the sofa and kicking off her shoes in the living room. I take the bag from the bathroom and stuff down into the kitchen bin, before taking that bag out too and tying it in a knot. Carefully keep my face away from her, I tell Christiana I am heading down to the bins and if she replies I don't hear it.

Mama is back a little while later – she doesn't like being out if Christiana is at home alone, so on the days I am here she likes to go out, but never late. As she comes in, she scolds me for not replacing the kitchen bin bag and I say I wasn't thinking from where I am on the sofa, one arm around Christiana whilst she watches something on the TV that I have not paid any attention to.

What do I tell Mama? Nothing, tell her nothing, comes the answer again. Whatever happens to me I know she will be there for me, but right now I don't know what to say to her about chasing a good man away. She has not been happy with me since I told her that I am not seeing Simon any more, and whilst I tried to explain why all she could do was tut and shake her head at me, saying she didn't understand what I meant about being in love, what did that even mean anyway, he was, is, a good man and kind and you can see it in his eyes so what is the matter with you?

Oh my God. What do I tell Simon? We have barely spoken at all since that night in his flat, except to do with handing over the ward so that he could go back to the Emergency room. I know he always loved working there before and I was pleased for him to be able to do so again, but I couldn't have the conversation about how happy I am for him. He deserves good things to happen for him. I haven't dared text him and he has not texted me either. I know I hurt him, so I am not surprised, but I did it for what I thought were the right reasons – but now this? How do I go back to him and tell him this? How do I say that I have his child growing inside me? How do I tell him that no matter what I am going to have this child, his child, now that we are not together?

Christiana has been talking to me for a couple of minutes and I have not responded – it takes a sharp elbow in the ribs to get me to focus on her. All she wants to know, though, is what is for dinner and when is it coming, and Mama who has been bustling around in the way that she always does is on hand to provide the answers when I don't have a clue. I drift off again but not before being skewered by a look from Mama accompanied by another shake of the head. I suspect that she hopes I am thinking over what I have done and regretting it, and I am, but not for the reasons she thinks I should.

I say nothing at work until I begin to show. To be honest, those uniforms – I still wear mine even though I am the manager at the moment – are not the most flattering or figure hugging so I could probably get away with it for longer, but when I see myself in the bathroom mirror and can see the unmistakable bulge beginning, I call Matron Wilshire and let her know. She is congratulatory and tells me that she has been meaning to call me anyway to offer me the manager job long term. We have a discussion over whether I want to leave a formal announcement until after the baby, but I tell her no, and ask her to keep the pregnancy confidential for now. She agrees sounding puzzled.

I tell Mama that night. She scoffs at me and tells me that she knows already and has known for weeks, did I think she was both blind and stupid? I tell her I did not think she was blind or stupid but if she knew why didn't she say anything?

"It was for you to work out what you wanted to do and when to tell me, Alina – you always know your own mind and do what you think is best, so advice from an old woman would make no difference any way. Does he know?"

I shake my head.

She tuts again and heads off to the kitchen without another word.

I sit Christiana down that night too and tell her – she is initially excited at the prospect of a baby sister – she has no doubt it will be – but begins to question where on earth this baby can have come from, and I remember I never told her about Simon, and she has never met him either. I try to explain sensitively without making it sound like her Mum got pregnant from a one-night stand which is why she never got to meet Mum's boyfriend, which is difficult. She does not accept that I could possibly have had a months-long relationship that not only did she not know about, but that I also kept it a secret from her, her primary reasoning being if I had been seeing him for months how could I not have told her about him? I have to do a lot of apologising before, during and after dinner that night and by the end I am not certain that she is convinced that I am telling the truth. It takes Mama to chip in about the nice man I brought home to dinner one night for Christiana to begin to believe that I might be telling the truth, but then Mama helpfully adds how I then pushed him away. Christiana is utterly outraged.

"So that's my baby sister's Dad?"

"Yes, it was. There hasn't been anyone else."

"I didn't know there was THIS one. Are you going to go and get him back?" she demands.

"No, I don't think so"

"Well, why not?"

"That's a very good question", Mama unhelpfully adds over her shoulder from the sink.

A good question, and I don't have a good answer except to say that what's done is done. Both Mama and Christiana tut at this, and I discover that my daughter is inheriting traits from my mother that I would rather she didn't, like a very disapproving view of me when it suits.

Unsatisfied, Christiana stomps off to her bedroom and I don't see her for the rest of the night, and to be honest the withering looks from Mama every time she passes are exhausting too, so I head to bed earlier than I planned to.

The next day I have to be at work but when I get home, I have to field a lot of questions from Christiana about what Simon is like, starting with his name, what he does ("Is he really a nurse? I thought women were nurses, are you sure he's not a doctor?"), what he looks like, is he rich, does he have a big enough car, does he have any other children, does that mean he'll have to be my Dad too now, is he married is that why you split up with him, will the baby have to live with him and a host more questions that I both can't remember and didn't have the answers to.

She is very disappointed at my lack of either information or prescience and sulks for most of the evening until she asks me if she can listen to the baby. I tell her she is not going to hear anything, but she is insistent until I let her lay on my belly, her ear pressed to it intently listening. After a few moments she leaps up smiling saying that she can hear the baby moving around in there. I don't have the heart to tell her that it is just my digestive system.

I still have no idea what I am going to do, so I carry on as normal except for getting bigger every day. Christiana's excitement builds and the subject of the baby's father doesn't come up, but the question of where the baby will sleep does. Mama softens towards me and starts knitting, everything in blue – when I ask her why she just gives a short laugh and points a knitting needle at my belly. I carry on making no plans at all – I don't know what I am thinking here, whether I believe some magical solution will materialise or what, but until I speak to Simon I can't make a plan, and I still haven't spoken to Simon yet.

As time moves on it becomes increasingly difficult to have the conversation with Simon, not just because of the time but because I know that he has started seeing Ella on my unit – she told me about it whilst we were making beds together one day – and I told her that I was pleased for them both. She seemed to be relieved and let out a breath that she seemed to have been holding in all morning. By this time there is no doubt, shoddy uniform or not, that I am heavily pregnant, and the ultrasound tells me that I have about six weeks to go. I haven't seen or heard from Simon in all that time and the longer it goes on the more difficult it is going to become to have that conversation but hearing that he and Ella are together now has just made having that conversation a whole lot more difficult, and I realise the folly of leaving it for as long as I have to say anything.

In the end it isn't really my choice to let him know. The Emergency department is slammed, and they are asking for the wards to come and collect patients rather than the usual way that they do the transfer. As my other two nurses are neck deep in drug rounds and leg dressings I agree to go and collect a patient who has been on the floor at home all night after a fall she couldn't get up from. As I waddle onto the unit I see him straight away – shirt sleeves rolled up, dark blue tunic on – as he turns, catches sight of me, smiles his smile, then almost immediately I see the colour drain from his face and in the middle of a packed room, his mug of tea fall from his hand and smash all over the floor.

Ella

I can't believe that things have gone as well as they have. After that night at the pub Simon and me text each other a lot and met up whenever we could — we go to dinner, we go to the movies, we go to the pub with and without Anna and Grace, he cooks me dinner a couple of times and I get to see his flat. He stays over at mine, and I stay over at his. I have this feeling inside me that is not at all like Sepp and I feel more comfortable with him than I have with any other person, but although we start sleeping together, we don't start *sleeping* together. It is not even like I have to rebuff him, we are intimate, and he is a caring and considerate of me and he gives me my first ever orgasm, a delicious and literally back arching experience, but actual sex still seems an obstacle for me.

Anna calls me almost daily for updates, and I tell Sabine (and, therefore, Olek, and most likely Sabine's entire circle of friends whether they know me or not) that I am dating a man called Simon and that yes, he is a nice man, and I don't need to go into too much detail as I am confident that she has already had plenty of detail from Anna. I tell Mama as well, and again suspect that Grace has got there first, especially as she speaks to Mama far more frequently than I do, and Mama almost seemed to be expectant of the news. Mama seems happy for me; I can almost hear her smile down the phone.

Obviously, I don't share the most intimate details of our relationship with either Sabine or Mama, but Anna seems to think that this is the most essential information of all and does not appear satisfied with whatever level of information I give her. Partly, though, I am not sure what to say. She knows enough about me that she knows I have never been overly keen on the physical side, which she has always found to be a little bizarre. Living with her has demonstrated that she is a big fan of the physical side of being in a relationship. The problem is that I am not sure how to explain how things are because to start with I am not sure that I understand them myself.

The thing is, he doesn't seem to mind, and I mean mind at all that we are not having sex. This bothers me so much that I decide to bring it up one day and bluntly tell him that I do want to fuck him one day, but I don't know when. He tells me that that is completely fine, that that will be in my own time, and I am not sure that I can bring myself to believe him, but later we still go to bed together, we are still intimate, and he still makes me climax with his touches and his mouth. Of course, it isn't a one-way street, I know the kinds of things men want, but for a change I find myself wanting to do those things for him. With Simon it feels like there has been a banked down fire inside me sometimes and I do want to have sex with him so badly some days, but just can't quite bring myself to do it.

It is a June day when the dam breaks. I have been sunbathing outside is just my underwear – my house has a little garden with high fences – when I hear the front door go. For a change a have what I would call a sexy set of purple underwear on, but what, if Anna's laundry basket is anything to go by, perhaps most people would say are nothing special – but I feel good in them. I have been expecting him and left the door on the latch expressly for him to let himself in and I hear him calling out for me to see if I am home. He is a little earlier than I expected but this is not so unusual – when he can get off work early to come and spend some time together, he will do – so I am not surprised. I get up from my towel and can feel and see that I am covered in a light sheen of sweat from the sun. I pad barefoot in through the patio door just as he enters the living room from the other side.

"You look hot" he says, smiling at his own little joke.

I don't know what triggers it – perhaps it was the hot sun – but something clicks inside my head, and I know that this is the time.

I stride purposefully over to him – with my long legs I am an impressive strider and I would think in my underwear an impressive sight – and I kiss him passionately and deeply on the mouth whilst I start pulling roughly at his shirt buttons. I hear one rip and land somewhere on the wooden floor and I don't care. He gets the hint and undoes a couple before pulling the whole thing off over his head, by which time I am already pulling at his belt buckle. I can feel his passion rising for me as I struggle with the buckle, button and zipper, before he helps me and pulls his trousers down and kicks them away, along with his shoes and socks. I pull down his pants and push him down onto the rug, so he is laying naked on his back and take him into my mouth. I look up into his eyes as I luxuriate in the pleasure, using my lips, my tongue, to his obvious excitement.

He is trying to reach for me to touch me, but it is only my head that is within reach so instead he throws his head back in mild frustration. In one move I pull off my own pants and straddle him, gasping in both surprise and pleasure as I push myself down hard on him – it has never felt like this before! – generating a gasp of surprise in him too. He looks up at me both stunned and inflamed with an obvious desire for me, and I can see in his eyes how much he has wanted me for so long.

He wanted me! Me!

Well, now he can have me.

He sits up and moves my legs so that they are wrapped around his waist, and I am sitting in his lap, still enclosing his manhood completely, and I instinctively begin to thrust myself on it. Our kisses are hotter and more passionate than ever they have been, I cannot get enough of the taste of his lips, and I bite him on the lip hard as one thrust sends a wave of ecstasy crash through me. I am sliding back and forth on his lap, our lips barely apart as we kiss almost primitively - we are being driven on by nothing more than our basest drives, there is no higher thought or reason here, this is animalistic, necessary, needed, inevitable. There is nothing outside this moment here, the two of us, there is no world and nothing in it expect Simon and me, and we are not flesh, nothing but feelings exist.

He has made me cum before, and I know it is coming, but never has it built up to feel like this and never can anyone have felt like this. When it comes, I feel like I am being torn apart, fibre by fibre, and thrown back together with all my nerves on the outside – every moment, every movement, every touch, feels amplified. My spine contorts and my mouth opens, and I scream and shudder.

It is not enough. It can never be enough, I can never have enough, and his passion for me is not ended either – I look into his beautiful brown eyes, and he looks into mine. We are searching each other's faces for something previously unknown, and I see it in him, I see it and I want it and I never want to lose it. We move slower, but not lessening the exquisite feeling I have inside, and I know I am going to cum again. I can hear a noise coming from somewhere and I realise it is me – a sort of sobbing, squeaking noise that I can't stop myself from making, nor do I want to. I am lost in these sensations, I am lost in this man, I am lost and I never want to be found again. He cries out and shudders beneath me and I feel his explosion inside me which thrills me and makes my spine twitch again. I hold him tightly to me, I am exhausted, and listen and feel as our breath is ragged and returns to normal. We are both soaked in sweat, but I feel no cold, I cling onto him with my fingers, my arms and my legs, I cling on to him inside me, my head on his shoulder, his on mine.

"I love you" I tell him, and this is the first time I have said these words to him.

"I love you" he rasps.

We sit like that, holding each other, long after our breathing has returned to normal, and our sweat has dried. I never want to let go.

"I never want to let go" I whisper.

"Then don't" he replies.

Alina

Anyone who might have had the slightest idea that we had been together – and, therefore, who the father of my baby is – would have had their suspicions confirmed there and then. However, Simon is convincing at explaining that as he turned toward the door to see me coming in, he knocked his hand against the terminal stand and his staff hurry around to help him clean up and, importantly – because I know, and they must know, how much he likes his tea – get him another mug of tea.

His composure recovers almost instantly, and he will not let me do the patient escort ("you must be out on your feet!") and there are a couple of willing volunteers to do the patient transfer themselves – probably to get out of the bedlam for a few minutes. He offers to let me sit down in his office for a few minutes and I accept – not just because I now have to have that talk with him, but because, truthfully, I suddenly do feel out on my feet.

He shows me to the door and opens it telling me to sit anywhere, before turning and heading back to the terminal he had been at. There isn't a lot to choose from in terms of seating, and his office is not nearly the size of the one on my ward, seemingly not much more than a re-purposed supply cupboard, but behind his small desk there is a good size and comfortable looking chair with a high back, and I gratefully collapse into it after throwing my cardigan over the back of the other non-descript chair, to find that the comfy looking one reclines as well. I feel a little like my legs are swinging in the air – Simon is so much taller than I am – but it is at least as comfortable as it looks and it is a welcome relief. It is longer than I thought it would be before Simon appears, and I am almost on the point of leaving when he comes in apologising.

"I can see you're busy" I say

"I can see you have been too" he says and immediately looks like he regrets it. I am a little offended by this, but I pause before I reply as I can see his point of view – I dump him for no good reason in his view, then turn up very pregnant. Crap reason + pregnant = someone else involved.

"It's yours, Simon." This comes out colder than I would have liked – but his comment did hurt. I realise that if we carry on like this it will not be a conversation that goes well, so I soften my tone a little.

"I am sorry, Simon – I didn't know, and by the time I did it was already so long and too hard to say anything, and I knew about Ella..." I trail off as he stands there looking for all the world like a lost little boy. His mouth is open and he is intermittently shaking his head in disbelief. I get up from the chair and go over to him to hold his hand.

"This is a lot and the wrong time, I know, but we need to talk about it. Can we talk later?" I ask.

He doesn't answer immediately, and I am about to say something else along the lines of getting back to the ward when he squeezes my hand holding his.

"I loved you, Alina. Hell, I do love you – however hard I try I can't stop. If you had just told me…" it is his turn to trail off.

"I'm with Ella now" he says.

"I know"

"Why didn't you tell me?"

I just look down and shake my head. I don't have a good reason – or even a bad one.

"How long?"

"Six weeks"

"Do you know what it is?". I don't and I shake my head again. He squeezes my hand again and then suddenly takes me, unresistingly, into his arms and hugs me. I don't think it is a romantic gesture but good God, I needed it. We embrace for a few seconds and separate, but I hold onto his hand again afterwards as he slumps into the other chair.

"You hurt me, Alina." He is not looking at me as he says this, his gaze seemingly fixed on the floor. "I thought we were good together."

"Simon? Simon, look at me. Please?" I put my hand gently under his chin and lift his head as he looks up at me "I am sorry, Simon, you didn't deserve to be hurt and I did – do – love you very much," he squeezes my hand again at this, "and I should have spoken to you sooner, I know, but this isn't the right time or place. Can we talk later?"

He nods, then stands, then hugs me again. I retrieve my cardigan and have my hand on the door handle as he says "Tonight", and it isn't a question. I pause, and I don't dare look back, before I nod once, and as fast as my overburdened legs will take me head back to the ward, closing the door behind me.

There is a little bit of fuss when I get back there – obviously, they were not expecting the patient to come up without me – so I say that I just felt a little unwell down in the Emergency room and had to sit down for a while. To my dismay I am told that I look terrible, and I am ushered to a chair at the nurses' station, where the ward clerk leaps up to get me a coffee and I am told in a motherly fashion that I am not to even attempt any more transfers today, and to sit there and drink my coffee until I feel better.

I plan to.

It plays heavily on my mind, though, how the conversation with Simon is going to go tonight. I wonder for a moment whether he is rehearsing what might be said, but then dismiss that as I recall an Emergency room packed full of people and noise, Simon at the centre of it, directing everything like some sort of ringmaster. There will be no time for brooding for him and knowing him as I do that is probably for the best. Of the many things I could say about Simon, focussed is one.

That brings me back to the conversation — albeit brief — that we have just had, though. I told him I love him, and I realise that this is true. As much as I have made a habit of keeping my thoughts to myself, and should not have told him that, I could not stop the words from coming out because of the undeniable weight of truth that they have. I do love him, and like him, although I wish I didn't and have tried to stop, I can't.

I do love him very much — and I realise that everything that I have done to protect me has really cut me deeper than I had anticipated or even believed would have been possible. It was so good to see him again, those first few seconds before he saw me, standing tall, and serious, and in his element, and almost invulnerable — the centre of attention not because he wants it but because he was needed and respected. I remember the early days before I really knew him and remember that that was how I saw him then, too, and how much, although I tried to deny it to myself, I had liked him for it. Then later, knowing that despite the persona that there was — damn it, is — a good, kind, gentle and caring man at the centre of it that I threw away to try and deny the truth of the matter, which was that I was in love, truly in love, for the first time in my life.

Realising these things break my heart and I begin to see what all this must have done to him too, and why, although I have told myself that I have had no explanation for not seeking him out sooner, that in reality I knew all along that I had been disastrously wrong about so many things and that seeing him again would bring that home – at least on that my subconscious was right.

And now, here I am, cold coffee in hand, on an uncomfortable office chair, feeling like I am in slow motion whilst everyone around moves faster and faster, doing everything I can to stop myself from sobbing uncontrollably as the weight of the mistakes and the weight of the feelings I have tried so hard to dampen down are washing over me.

Ella

"No"

"What do you mean no?"

"I mean no – I don't agree with you."

Simon looks at me with a puzzled expression on his face.

We have been at this for what seems to have lasted an eternity but in reality, can have been no more than half an hour at the most, and Simon looks absolutely exhausted, as well as having red-rimmed eyes and now, an expression of absolute bewilderment.

His mouth opens and closes making the sounds like the beginning of sentences, but not getting as far as forming an actual word.

"I mean no, Simon. I told you that I don't want to let go, and you told me that I never have to. So, I'm not."

"But Ella!" He is almost pleading now. "I am going to be a father! I have to be there for the baby, I can't..." He trails off. There are a few more false starts, and it is clear he is trying to find the right words to say. This may be a little unfair of me as I am not entirely sure that there are many, if any right words, but he made a promise to me and I see no reason for him not to keep it – the last half an hour has been him breaking the news to me that he is going to be a father, that the mother is Alina, and that these two facts on their own are enough for him to leave me – and as far as I am concerned, they most certainly are not.

"I'm going to be a father, and I have every intention to be there for my child – supporting it, and yes, supporting Alina too. I have no idea what being a single mother to a new baby must be like and I am not going to let that happen to my child!"

"I'm not asking you to!"

"But I don't understand! How can I be there – wherever there is! – with my child and the mother of my child and be here with you too!"

I don't like seeing Simon like this – he is usually so in control, he usually looks like there is nothing in the world that can phase him, so I do have some sympathy for how he must be feeling right now, because I can see that all this has come as a huge shock to him and that his world has been rocked by this...revelation, but I am not going to let it look like this is a huge shock to me – although it genuinely is – or that this changes anything at all for me, because it doesn't.

What he does not yet understand – and I have only just begun to – is that for the first time in my life I can have let myself feel. I am beginning to think that the whole of my life I have kept everything that even looks like a feeling at arm's length, I have never let myself feel for someone – especially not a man! – in the way that I do now. Before, whatever I was, whatever I did, was because I had a space that someone else wanted me to fit into, there was no space for what I wanted or how I felt – except for with Sabine and Olek. With them I could be whoever I wanted to, and looking back I enjoyed living with them, having Sabine and Anna to chat to whenever I wanted, my own space whenever I wanted, and looking after Diane.

They gave me that space, but now, I have allowed myself the room, the permission to feel things and Simon has been the one has helped make that possible. I have created my own spaces and this one fits me best because it is me. Simon has never expected anything from me except for me to be myself, he has always taken me for who I am not for whom he wants me to be. Part of this argument, such as it is, is because now I owe him the same. I realise that where I needed his support to be me, now he needs my support to be him.

"Simon, my love, you made me a promise." I am talking to him quite calmly – because, I am surprised to find, I am. "You made me a promise – you said I never have to let go. So, I won't. Wherever you are, my love, I will be there with you."

"What about Alina?"

"Alina will have to understand. I have no problem with you supporting your family, but what she will have to understand is that I am part of your family too."

And it is as I say these words that I realise them to be true.

He shakes his head at this, as though he can't quite believe that what I am saying, but there it is, there laid out for him is what I feel about him.

"Do you want to be with me?" I ask, lowering my head a little and praying to God for the right answer. Fortunately, he gives it to me.

"Of course I do – just because this has happened hasn't changed how I feel about you." He says this with some tenderness which is a lot better to hear than pleading, and he sounds more like the Simon I have fallen in love with than he did a minute ago. "I just don't know how we can make it all work in the way that you're saying."

I needed to hear him say that he wants me. I am not sure what I would have done if there was any hesitation or catch in his voice. I have opened myself to having feelings – I realise in that moment that it would have broken me if they were not returned.

"We'll have to find a way, my love, because I am not letting you go."

"You've made that clear, darling girl," and as he says this, he reaches out for me, and I fall gratefully into his arms to be held softly. He kisses the top of my head and I snuggle into him a little tighter.

Right here is where I want to be, always. Here I feel at home.

We agree – well, kind of agree, because I can see that Simon still isn't too sure about all of this – that we will both go and meet Alina next time, so that everyone knows where they stand. He is supposed to be meeting with her tonight, but he agrees to call her and reschedule – he tells her that he has to get his head around a few things first. I have had to be a little more robust with Simon than I am used to being and it does make me feel uncomfortable to have to put my foot down with him like this, but I have my reasons.

It is so that I can get to her first.

I tell both Anna and Grace about my plan at the pub the following night – they are outraged, and both think I am insane, but to me this is the most sensible thing in the world.

I try to explain to them both – and I think that Anna might even understand it a little by the end – that I have lived for so long letting other people define me and define where I fit in the world, so when I have found the right person, the right fit, and for once, for once feel comfortable, it is like a weight lifted off me that I have carried for my whole life and I can breathe, and that I am not going to let it go – not now, and not ever.

Dee

It is true what Sarah said – Ben is a man that deserves love. He is kind to me, takes care of me and can never do enough for me. We have spent the last few months planning our Grand European Tour and saving as much as we can as we will both be off work for several months. We have decided to tour in a camper van and ended up spending a bit more money on that than we had planned, so have had to delay the departure for a bit – and that was mostly my fault, I was determined to have at least a measure of comfort that our original budget did not allow for.

This time spent with Ben has been good for both of us, I think – where before my attention was always divided, unevenly and unfairly, now we have a joint project to concentrate on. We have become closer again, back almost to a point before Simon ever existed in my world. Now, I barely even think of him, although some months ago I did call him for a catch up and heard everything about the new girlfriend, presumably the one after the bad break-up girl. He sounded happy – maybe he'll be able to do, now, those things that he talked about, like making a family. Of the things I have never wanted in my life top of the list has been a child, so I am happy to think of him being happy at the prospect of something that I would never have been able, nor ever wished, to provide. No doubt soon he will have a nice house and a nice girlfriend and, I'm quite sure, a handsome baby and a life that suits him, but that life would not have ever suited me.

Whilst our sex life – Ben's and mine – has never been spectacular, we have struggled to bring back something even approaching our pre-Simon days, but it has become a part of our lives again. Ben is – as he is with everything to do with me – a kind and attentive lover and can never to enough for me, but he would be the first to admit – if anyone dared ask him and he had the courage to reply – that he is an inexpert lover, but where before this would have caused some resentment, and a text message at the very least to Simon, I have worked hard to curb my selfishness and try to enjoy these times for Ben's sake more than mine.

Back when I was seeing Simon, I would spend a lot of time paying a good deal of attention to my own body – I liked touching my body, guided and unguided, stroking, caressing, and, yes, masturbating a lot, but with that chapter seemingly closed off now I have been much less inclined – so despite his lack of expertise, it is Ben that notices a problem first whilst we are in bed together one night. His hand stops moving sharply as he is he squeezing my breast and a look of puzzlement crosses his face.

"There's a lump", he says.

"What?" I say, sure that I have misheard him.

"A lump" he says, "I can feel it."

I sit up sharply, smack his hand away and start feeling for myself. "I can't feel anything!". I remember giving him an accusatory look.

"It's there Denise, honestly, I'm sure of it!"

I flicked the light on, threw the covers off the bed and leapt up to stand in front of the wardrobe mirror, left arm bent over my head, right hand working from the nipple outwards, small circles...and it is there, at the four o'clock position, a hard lump and...yes, ouch... a little painful when I press on it.

I take my hand away and try again – yes, same position, a hard lump. I do it again to check again and press on it again and yes, again, there is a hard painful lump in my left breast.

Ben has said nothing whilst I do this and has done nothing except sit up in bed and look worried. When I turn to look at him, I can see that he has got both hands clasped together in front of him like he is praying, although he is just looking at me.

"I'm sure it's nothing.", I hear myself say, and although I am probably trying to reassure me more than him, he does seem to unwind a little. I have the thought that really it should be him that is doing the reassuring. I get back into bed and sex is most definitely no longer an option, for either of us. Ben lays back down and I put the light out. He doesn't even try to cuddle me but turns on his side facing away.

I don't know what I am expecting him to say or do, but to say and do nothing seems a little harsh, I think. After some time, I hear him fall asleep but I think there is little chance of that happening for me. I lay on my back in the darkness re-examining my left breast over and over, until it begins to feel quite abused, and I try to sleep myself, but it is not coming.

I called in sick for my next day at work and arranged to see my GP that afternoon. To be honest, I would have been of no use to the lab – I fell asleep at some point but can have been for no more than an hour or two at best. My GP finds the lump straight away and I endure some more robust pushing and prodding.

"It's hard", she says, "and irregular if I am any judge". I know that this is not good news. "I'll arrange for an urgent oncology assessment. On the other hand, it could just be an abscess or a benign lump – women do get those too." I know this kind of stuff – you don't work in a hospital laboratory without picking up a few things. She asks me to lift my arm again and presses hard in my armpit.

"How long have you had that swelling in your armpit?" she asks. I tell her I didn't know I had one there too, and when she has finished examining me, I put my own hand there and can feel another lump there as well. Again, I know enough to know that this is a troubling sign, and I say so.

Dr. Weir has taken off her gloves and is washing her hands.

"Well, it still could be benign or an infection – a piece of an infection might have travelled to the axilla and produced another abscess there as well, or the other way around, but yes, that is troubling." She sits back down at her desk and tells me to get dressed again. By the time I have she is well into completing the patient record on the computer and making referrals. She draws blood to send to the lab – possibly even to my lab – so that the oncologist will have results by the time the appointment arrives. She tells me to see her urgently if I have any more symptoms or call if I have any questions. I don't call because there are no questions I have that I haven't already got the answers for.

The next few weeks, starting within just a few days of the GP appointment, are a hail of repeated embarrassing and painful tests – mammograms of both breasts, physical examinations, blood tests, appointment after appointment, and biopsies of the two lumps. I start not bothering to wear a bra to appointments – even though I could use the support – because I know that every time I have go somewhere I end up having to get undressed and dressed again, so it saves time. Ditto wearing either a loose vest or baggy jumper. More people get to see my tits in those few short weeks than have in my entire life. And of course, it is all done with such sensitivity and kindness, and everything is done with the minimum necessary exposure, I get that, but still it is a problem with my tits so I have to keep getting them out all the time.

The news when the consultant gives it to me is of no real surprise. Cancer. Tumours in both the left breast and the lymph node in the axilla. Metastasised. Probably lung involvement, further biopsies needed. Poor differentiated. Malignant. Imminent treatment. Chemotherapy. These and other words wash over me as I sit in the uncomfortable clinic chair in my shitty baggy jumper and jeans. I feel like I am having an out of body experience, the room, and the people in it seem unreal to me. I am barely picking out one word in three. Then she says a word that snaps me right back into reality.

Mastectomy.

Ben has been with me to none of the appointments or tests – to be honest, I know that I would have to hold his hand for him, rather than the other way around. He did offer the first few times, but I could see the relief in his face when I gently declined – I could almost see his shoulders bunched up around his ears as he would work his way up to asking me if I wanted him to come with me and see them descend again when I would politely decline. I know that I am going to have to tell him about this, that I am going to have to tell him that the next few months are going to be a brutal surgery followed by being drip fed poisons that will make me bald, or nauseated to the point of preferring starvation to eating, or both; exhausted to the point of desperate for release, any release, or depression to the point of suicidal ideation, or both, that to manage the pain and the chemo side effects I am going to have to take a small pharmacy of drugs every day, and likely to be so knocked off by them that I can barely stay awake.

Ben is a good man, but he does not have the stomach (ha!) for this. I'm going to need more than the superficial fun-time girl that Becca would like to be can provide. I'm going to need more proximity than someone raising their family in the West Indies can give me over a weekly Skype call. My Mother will be my Mother and try and take over everything, but lacks even the knowledge that I have about these things to understand more than a fraction of what is going on.

Examining the alternatives, I can see that there are surprisingly few, and only one that is slightly less worse than the others. I am genuinely equivocal about this – I don't want to do this for several reasons, not least of which I will be turning up feeling that I am damaged and/or incomplete, but I can see that there is only one logical alternative, one and only one person that I can lean on to get me through all of what is to come. I wait for Ben to go to work – after he has asked me roughly thirty times if I will be ok ("no, Ben, I will not be OK" is what I want to say, but I don't) – then I pull out the largest suitcase that we had bought for the Europe trip, fill it with only comfortable clothes and drag it to the car. I don't pack makeup, perfume, toiletries and all that rubbish – I pack my toothbrush, of course, I'm not an animal – because what would be the point of all that crap? It's not like I am planning to enter any beauty pageants for the rest of my life, and I am not sure that a bit of lippy is going to disguise the fact that I am going to turn into a skeletal, depressed, puking, one titted, bald half-dead zombie. I am not getting on the cover of Vogue any time soon.

I have the presence of mind to delete the tracking app before I leave.

I am genuinely doing Ben a favour – I don't know why he has stayed by me all this time, but I do know that he hasn't done it so that he can wipe vomit off me. He has deserved better than I have been to him and does not deserve this too. I am too young to be facing my mortality and so is he – but that also means that he is young enough to start over, begin afresh. I know that I am sounding like a hard-hearted bitch, even to myself, but I also know the reality of what I am facing which Ben, frankly, doesn't. I love him enough not to do this to him as well, and I know he won't see it like that but one of us has to be grounded in reality, one of us has to take a hard look at the situation and work out what is the better option.

My better option, out of all the crap options I have, is Simon, the one person I know that can handle what is coming, the one person who will have any insight into what it ahead, the one person who (hopefully) cares enough about me to take care of me when I need it and leave me be when I don't. I find the address he sent me and put it in the sat nav. I don't call because it will be a lot harder to turn away a dying woman on the doorstep than it will be over the phone. I know, I know, cold and calculating – but when you are on your last hope, you'll do everything you can to make it work too, I'll bet. Judge me when your back is against the wall.

I arrive at his flat in the early afternoon to find that he has gone. Left. Disappeared. After several fruitless minutes banging on the door, ringing the bell and looking through the window – thank God he is on the ground floor otherwise I am sure I'd be looking for a ladder right now – I realise that the 'For let' sign I saw outside was for this flat, his flat. I can feel a sob of anger and frustration struggling to make itself heard, and it has almost made it out into the world – my knees begin to buckle, and I wonder for the first time what I must look like, frantically banging on doors and peering through windows to an empty flat, when a timid voice says, "Excuse me, are you OK?".

I turn to see a woman whose whole demeanour matches the voice, right down to the big round glasses and pink cardigan. I self-consciously brush my hands on my jeans to get rid of the lichen and brick dust from where I have been leaning on the window ledge and as I do so I look down and realise that I have come out in a pair of slippers that have not handled tramping through damp ankle height grass well. Fuck my life.

"Are you looking for Simon?" she squeaks. I nod. "He's moved out", she says, then adds helpfully "about six month's ago."

"I don't suppose he left a forwarding address, did he?"

She brightens as she clearly has just remembered that he did just that. "OH, I'll get it!". She turns to leave before turning back and adding tentatively, "Do you...er...want to come in while I find it?"

"No, no, that's fine, just the address."

"Ok, I'll be back in a flash."

True to her word she is back quickly and five minutes later I am back at the car with a scrap of paper clutched in my hand with a beautifully printed address on it – she has obviously copied this out for me, because this is nothing like his handwriting. I rummage through my suitcase and find a pair of sneakers and change out of my sodden slippers, throwing them with some frustration and anger into the car as I do. I get back behind the wheel and compose myself – that sob of anger has been contained. I sweep back my hair from my face and pull it into a rough ponytail – there's always a bobble round the gearstick for just these occasions – and set off again.

Alina

I am only a little surprised when I see Ella march onto the ward when she is not on duty and make a beeline for me. I can see that she is vibrating like a violin string and, just like a violin string, looks taut enough that I think if I were to put the lightest of physical pressure on her, she would snap.

"We need to talk", she says, and the vibration has not ended with her body, it is in her voice too. She seems more nervous than angry, and I had certainly expected angry. I nod, close the patient file I had open on the counter, and lead the way to the office. I feel like I am being watched by everyone on the ward but I am pretty sure that that is just me, after all, it is not so unusual to see off duty staff on the ward wanting to speak to me about their rota or leave or whatever, and it isn't like the office is miles away from reception anyway, but I do feel more comfortable once we are both in the office and away from prying eyes. Ella strides right past me and sits down, and I sag with my back against the door for a moment, before I go and sit in my chair.

I look at her in the chair for a moment as I squeeze – and it is a squeeze – past my desk and I imagine that that is what I must have looked like to Simon, way back when. She is hunched forward looking at the floor, hands clasped together, although unlike me she has very short hair, so her face is not covered. I note that she looks almost deathly pale, and that she is chewing on her bottom lip. I am convinced that my original judgement that her tension is charged by nervousness is the right one.

I sit down and wait for her to speak – as well as seriously worrying her bottom lip, she looks like she is alternately trying to twist off each of her thumbs.

The silence is getting to the point of being uncomfortable, and I clear my throat as though to speak, when she seems to take this moment to address the floor.

"Do you love him?" It is very quiet and a little mumbled, and I have to do a little interpretation – she emphasises 'love' and I hear the rising tone of a question, so I make a bit of an assumption.

"Yes," I say, "yes I do." I say this calmly, even though I don't feel particularly calm – but then I have had a lifetime, it seems, of staying calm around emotional people.

She looks up at me and her pale blue eyes seem to be scanning me for any sign of deception.

"Well, I do too." She says this almost like a challenge, and when no challenge is returned goes back to talking to the floor.

"You can't take him away from me," she continues, "and he made me a promise."

"I never said I wanted to take him..."

"He is a good man, you know." She looks up at me again.

"I know"

Her head drops again, and her hands are pale in patches where her fingers are pressing into her own skin.

"I know" I repeat, and wish that I hadn't sat behind this desk, I must be coming across as cold, so I try and inject some warmth and sensitivity into the words the second time.

"I am not letting go. I don't have to!" The last few words are said much more forcefully than anything else she has said so far, and she smacks the palm of her hand with her fist.

It is looking like another long silence might be coming, so I work my way out from behind the desk and pull up a chair next to her. I hesitantly reach out a hand to put it around her shoulders, almost pull it back, but then put my arm around her. She immediately bursts into tears and leans into me, sobbing.

"It's ok, it's ok," I find myself saying, and putting both my arms around her and shushing her like I would Christiana. The tears and sobs settle after a minute, and she rights herself in her chair.

"Don't you see? He is a good man!" she says whilst looking away and dabbing at her eyes with her sleeve. I must look puzzled because I don't see the connection between whether Simon is a good man or not and the two of them staying together. My lack of a response makes her turn to me again.

"He will want to be with the baby!"

"...and he can be when he wants, he is the baby's father and..."

"Do you even *know* Simon?"

I am a little taken aback, but Ella continues on.

"He is going to be a father to your baby. A father! Not a part time Dad, he is going to want to be there for the baby." She is looking at the floor again but adds "And for you" with a sharp glance in my direction.

"Well, isn't that up to Simon to decide?" I suggest. Her look makes it clear that this is not the correct conclusion in her view.

"He made ME a promise", which is stated like an inviolable fact, each word enunciated both clearly and determinedly. "I am not letting go. Not now and not ever."

"Well, that's fine too, isn't it?" I ask, "Simon can make his own mind up and..."

"NO!" she almost shouts. "No, he can't! I am not going to make him choose, and neither should you!"

Again, I must look puzzled.

"We have to make the decision! You and me! YOU broke his heart! YOU left him! YOU hid that" and she points at my belly "from him. But YOU are going to be the mother of his child. He won't choose you, but he will choose the baby and he will give up on love and YOU will make him break his promise to me for his baby because he is a good man! Doesn't he deserve to have love too?"

It's not anger that has been driving her, but there is a depth and strength of feeling that has been banked down but has now spilled over. She takes a deep breath and banks the fire down again.

"He will want to be with his child, and that is fine and right, but he should be with me too." She adds more quietly "And I should be with him. I love him. And he loves me", she adds, looking up again with what borders on defiance.

She straightens in the chair again and seems to pull herself together. She dabs at her eyes with her sleeve again, sniffs petitely, and is clearly making an effort to compose herself. She places her palms with some exaggerated care on her knees.

"So...we are going to live together."

"I'm sure you'll be very happy..."

"All of us."

"All of who? I'm not sure who you're..."

"All of us." She is making a circular motion in the air with her index finger as though describing a giant lasso. "He can be there for the baby, and he can be there for you and me."

I am shaking my head. I have no idea what to say.

"Don't you see?"

"I don't know what to say, I really don't. See what?"

"Think about it – God knows that is all I have done since I found out, since Simon found out about the baby. I know that he loves you too, in his own way, and you said you love him, and I do too, and...". The words seem to be rushing out all at once, but I am still taking in what she is saying. All of us living together?

"All of us...living together?"

"Yes"

I can feel myself grasping for something to say. I stammer and splutter "Where?!", as much to give myself time to think as anything. All of us, living together.

And I can hear a little voice inside that keeps saying "But why not?"

"Does it really matter right now? I don't know where, but we will find something. This is why I came to you with this, not just so that neither of us lose, but so that we can work together. I used to be an au pair, you know". This information appears to be imparted with no small amount of pride.

I am stuck for words again. I seems so crazy to me but when I try to think why it's crazy, I can't come up with anything, except "But why not?"

"I'll think about it."

"You have a day."

"What?!" I splutter again.

"Alina, that" she says pointing at my belly again "is not going to stay in there forever. You can take a day, then tomorrow night you can come to dinner at mine, and we will tell Simon what is going to happen."

"If I agree..."

"You will. It's the only sensible option."

She stands sharply to leave, so I do too. I am reeling from this conversation – I suspect that I probably look just like she did when she came in, pale and anxious.

Then she puts her arms around me and hugs me warmly – it is a bit awkward as she is taller than me and has to lean over my belly.

"It'll work" she says in my ear, whilst patting my back "you'll see. We'll look after each other."

As she breaks away, she nods – to herself or to me, I am not quite sure – as though she has done what she needed to do, and indeed, what else is there to say? Without ceremony she leaves the office with a little wave and a little smile at the door as she goes, although she does not seem to be any the less anxious than when she came in. I shake my head at her as the door closes behind her, but I still can't think of a single reason why her suggestion is not as crazy as it sounds. But why not? The rest of the day it is all I can think of, trying to find the flaw in Ella's plan. But why not? I send her a text to tell her about Mama and Christiana, and she replies to say she already knows because Simon had told her, and that it doesn't make any difference, we will just have to find a big house – which is then followed by a list of properties she has already found on the internet. I can't help feeling more than a little impressed that she has taken the time to do some planning, and then think back to the assumption that she made that I was going to agree.

But why not indeed? Why not?

Ella

The baby is asleep in my arms – I have been at Alina's side since she went into labour yesterday, and she is exhausted and asleep. Simon is out getting him and me a drink, but I don't hold out much hope for anything more than vending machine coffee – it is coming up to midnight. Alina has been asleep for an hour or so, her first rest, and although I have been awake for all that time too, I am nowhere near as fatigued.

The baby is asleep too, his little hand curled around my index finger. He has that same squidgy, pudgy face that all babies have, but I think he looks more like Alina than Simon – he is blond, for a start.

We had a difficult time getting the maternity unit let me in, but Alina insisted, and when Alina insists it is hard to turn her down, I have found. I think it helped that the matron knew, or at least recognised, Simon as someone important at the hospital and waved us through.

I have learned more Romanian swear words in the last day than I think I will ever need, and I have also learned that if this is what pregnancy and labour are like, I never want to have any part in it. This child is, though, perfect. Angelic, even. I feel such emotions towards him that I had never expected, this tiny life that I hold in my arms, and I know that he is now, and forever will be, my family.

Simon comes back into the room with the predicted vending machine coffee – I motion to him to be quiet, so he places a paper cup next to me and moves to the other chair in the other corner of the room. He sort of slides himself down in the chair so that his head can rest on the back, closes his eyes and puffs out his cheeks into a sigh. He looks as exhausted and drained as Alina does, but then he has been looking pretty much like that for the last four weeks, ever since dinner at mine.

Simon had come home a little later than usual, doing his usual thing when he is late of getting the explanation out of the way as he is coming in the door – an accident on the North Circular today, apparently – but he stopped sharply when he saw Alina there. Usually, Grace will stay out of the way if she knows Simon is coming over, but she was there too – whilst she was unsure of this plan at the start, she, Anna, and I have been discussing this plan for longer that either Simon or Alina and we think we have all the bases covered – she is here for my support. Simon's mouth had hung open for a moment, clearly never expecting two parts of his life to overlap and be in the same room at the same time.

I got up to kiss him and guided him to a dining chair. "You've timed it just right; dinner is almost ready." I patted him on the shoulder as he sat down and squeezed it gently – I am sure Alina saw this, and I wanted her to. She hid it by taking a sip of the sparkling water she had.

I went to the kitchen and brought back stew – nothing special, just meat, potatoes and some vegetables – to see that conversation was going to be difficult to get started, and begun to think that there was going to be some difficulty getting around to the subject in hand, but to his – and Alina's – credit, they did a good job of polite "how has your day been?" conversation. As he does whenever he sees her, he makes an effort to include Grace in the conversation and she tells him about her new job which she had started not long after that night at the pub together, and a new boyfriend she has been seeing for about the same time. Perhaps seeing me and Simon made Grace get out and do something for herself, but maybe it was just a coincidence.

As I sat there picking at my stew – my stomach was such a knot I was surprised I was even getting the wine I had down me – I could see more clearly than before that this could work, after all, here we all were, eating and drinking and talking together like it was the most normal thing.

The previous 24 hours had been fruitful; Alina had asked a lot of questions and I had done a lot of research into houses, and as time went on, I could sense that she was coming around to my way of thinking. We met up for coffee this morning so that we could plan this meal tonight and talk over some of the other details, like who was going to pay for what and how we were going to coordinate three homes moving into one. I had the ghost of Anna sitting on my shoulder all the time, though – whatever element of the plan we had discussed it was always Anna that played the protector, ensuring that I wasn't going too far or expecting too much. I think she would have liked to have been at that dinner, but in a way, I am pleased that she was not. I know she likes Simon, but I think that protectiveness would have been like a brick wall down the table between me, Simon, and Anna on one side and Alina on the other. As it was, conversation flowed and people relaxed – and as Simon mopped up the last of the stew from the pot with a hunk of bread, I began to tell him about what Alina and I had agreed on.

We did not give him an option, but then, he never looked like he wanted one, either. We set it all out, explained how this was the only way that made sense and how this way we would be a family together. Then, family meant much less to me than it does right now, holding this little life in my arms, but to be honest family has meant so little to me for such a long time.

Simon went through phases of shock, surprise, and bewilderment, but never baulked at the idea and by the end of the evening was even taking in interest in the work I had done to find the right place, although I could see that he was uncomfortable about being affectionate towards me, so I made an effort to sit closely to him or put my arm around his shoulders or kiss him on the cheek – now, though, I wonder whose benefit that had been for.

Anna had insisted on meeting Alina and did so that week, and typical of Anna she sized Alina up in about a second and decided that she quite liked her – and to be honest I can see many similarities between the two of them, they both dress better than I do for a start. Before long they were chatting and Anna was laughing at Alina's rusty French, which as it turned out she had spoken quite well at one time. With Anna's approval seemed to come Alina's friendship too, and unlike a lot of times when I am with Anna, I felt that I was a real part of the gang; it seemed to be that Alina was the conduit that was making sure that I was included.

What started out an arrangement of convenience between two people with shared interests – Simon – quickly became a friendship and trust between two women that would be there for each other. It had been a lot of work finding, arranging a let, packing, organising movers, and doing the actual moving, and throughout Alina and I seemed to become closer and more trusting of one another. Anna,

Grace and me had helped pack up her flat and had helped Mama and Christiana too – I was pleased to find her to be a lovely girl to me and very excited about moving to a big house. Alina told me later that Mama had said that I was too skinny and needed some of her cooking inside of me, which is approval of a kind I suppose.

I was in the middle of doing some of the unpacking whilst Simon and Alina were at work when Alina called. I resisted the temptation to revive the disagreement we had had to keep going to work so late in her pregnancy, and as close as we had become over the last few weeks, it did not occur to me as odd that it was me that she called first when she went into labour whilst she was on the ward. Now, recalling how I had stood up for what I wanted on the ward that day, I can reflect that this might not have been such a positive outcome – but I am very happy with how things have turned out.

I don't know what the other staff must have thought about me turning up to escort her to the maternity wing – although I suspect some of the less charitable ones thought no more than we were Eastern European women sticking together – and it made more sense for me to go than to send Simon because as far as they are concerned, he had nothing to do with Alina or her pregnancy. I had turned up with a wheelchair that I had found at the front entrance to the hospital, having texted Simon to meet us at the mat unit. As I helped her into the chair, she gripped my hand so tightly the skin went white.

"Don't leave me", she said through gritted teeth.

I promised her I wouldn't.

The mat unit sent her home at first, not being far enough along, so we met Simon coming in along the corridor as we were going out. We, well I, took her to our new home – such as it was, with packing boxes still unpacked and furniture not necessarily in the right place – and she had insisted that she travel with me, not Simon. Changing gears whilst she was having a contraction wasn't always easy as she would cling to my left arm as she breathed through it.

Between contractions she would sometimes look at me and repeat her plea, with varying degrees of emotion as the day went by. And I stayed by her side the whole way through, even going to the bathroom with her, helping support her when she felt like her legs would give way, rubbing her back and shoulders for her, following her around the house and the ward whispering encouragement, and later mopping her brow with a cool flannel and telling her what a good job she was doing, how it would be all over soon and encouraging to push. Simon was there but he did the running; making teas, finding, and packing a bag, timing the contractions, changing the flannel as needed, whatever she or I needed.

That's why I was sitting here, holding this small child whilst Simon was out looking for coffee. I might have been late to the party, but Alina and I have worked hard for this little boy over the last couple of days and I deserve it.

Alina and Simon want to call him Jack, and Alina asked me what I thought about that. I told them that I think that it suits him.

"Sleep well, Jack", I whisper to him, and kiss him gently on the forehead. He fusses a little but then goes back to sleep. No one else sees this – this is just for him and me.

Simon is already snoring.

...and sevens

Simon

I am leaning against the counter thinking about nothing much – the house is quiet this morning, as far as I can tell I am the only one up, so in the quiet I've become contemplative, and find myself reviewing the events of the last few months.

I am disturbed from this reverie by the noise of a car pulling up outside. From here in the kitchen, I can see our short driveway but there is nothing there, so I step up to the window to see a large black Volvo I don't recognise pulled up at the side of the road. The strange thing is that it looks like someone in uniform getting out of the driver's seat. The car itself obscures the driver partially until he comes around to the passenger side, but I can see what looks like a smartly dressed woman with a lanyard getting out of the passenger seat, looking up and down the street and checking something on her phone. By now I have seen the driver's police uniform as he holds the passenger door open for her – I reason that she is clearly a person of importance to be driven around by a police officer.

I am a little surprised when they both start walking up the path to my door and I am at the door holding it open by the time that they reach it.

"Mr Simon Holcroft?", she says. I just nod dumbly.

"Detective Chief Inspector Carol Deacon, this is Police Constable Allan, may we come inside?" She is holding up her lanyard ID which very clearly has a police crest on it, her name and her photo.

"Of course", I say, "Can I ask what this is about?"

"We are investigating the death of Denise Saunders. I believe she lived here until death" it's a statement, not a question "and I would like to ask you a few questions."

Dee

The house is much larger than I expected, and I begin to doubt whether I have the right place, rechecking the slip of paper given to me by the neighbour. I check the address and then the sat-nav, but it assures me that it has brought me to the right place.

The lights are on downstairs, and I can see an uncurtained window that I assume is for a kitchen – but I don't waste any time scrutinising it any closer, I get out of the car and go to the boot to get the suitcase. For some reason, even though I got the fucking thing into the boot, it doesn't want to come out, and I tug on it with anger and frustration until it is partially sitting on the edge of the boot, and partially overhanging. A sharp tug drops it edge down on the floor with a whump.

I close the boot and lock it. It's when I go to move the suitcase that I remember that the stupid fucking thing hasn't got any wheels, so I have to take the handle in both hands, pull it to my hip, and inelegantly wobble up to the door, which opens when I am about six feet from it.

And it is him – he is there, and I feel as though I am about to buckle when I see that he is not alone; to the side and slightly behind him is somebody in a scruffy pink dressing gown that, due to their diminutive size, reaches almost to the floor. For a moment I think she is a child but as I get closer, I see that it is a small woman who, as I look, takes hold of Simon's arm in both hands.

Simon has not moved or spoken.

I lower the suitcase at the doorstep and with my hand still resting on the handle, take a couple of deep breaths – the damn thing was heavy – and still no one has said anything.

I look from face to face and say "Hello, Simon".

"Dee?", he says. I am reminded of times when this word alone would have been accompanied by a broad smile. There is no broad smile.

He turns to the woman clinging to his arm. "Darling, this is... uh... Denise. She's... uh... an old friend." I hear the catches in his voice in this sentence. I'm sure his 'darling' does too. An old friend, huh? So that is what I have been reduced to. Mind you, that is exactly how I feel – old.

The woman introduces herself, in a heavily accented voice, the origins of which I don't recognise but would think Baltic somewhere, as Alina. She extends a hand and once we have shaken, returns it to Simon's arm. In the meantime, Simon is looking back and forth between me and the suitcase.

An uncomfortable silence descends, until Simon asks me if I'd like to come in. I say I do and pick up the suitcase again. Simon flattens himself against what must be a coatrack behind the door, and it is with no small satisfaction that, as I follow Alina behind and I struggle past him in the narrow hallway, I hear him 'Oof' as the suitcase catches him on the leg. There's a staircase and I drop the suitcase near the foot of it whilst Simon closes the front door behind me.

"Let's go through to the kitchen, shall we? There's coffee", he says. Alina shows me seat, a kind of barstool by a large rustic looking table and Simon makes for the coffee pot. Half an eye on me, Alina crosses the room and encircles his waist, before saying she must go and get ready. As he turns around to her, she tiptoes up to kiss him – a proper, full on mouth kiss, which is both inappropriate and deliberate in my view, excuses herself to me and leaves the room. I hear her on the stairs and then door closing upstairs as Simon hands me a steaming mug.

I look around at his is nice kitchen with gleaming chrome gadgets here and there, a wide ceramic sink, a new looking stove and ample room for this large table and barstools. He sits opposite me where he was clearly sitting when I arrived – there is an open newspaper and a half-eaten slice of toast next to him.

"Well?", I say, somewhat aggressively. "Aren't you going to say you're pleased to see me?"

"What do you want, Denise? And why have you brought a suitcase?"

"You've done alright for yourself, then – nice place, have you married into money then?"

I hadn't noticed before but as I say this, I look for a wedding ring – there isn't one.

"What" he says, pausing between the words, "do you want?"

"I need you, Simon."

"Oh, really?" – he is mocking in his tone, but quietly enough so that his voice won't carry much beyond the doorway. "You decide that you want me, so you turn up at my home... at my fucking *home*... with a suitcase? And I'm presume that you just expect to just move right in?" he hisses.

"You arrogant fucking arsehole!" I hiss back, angered by his tone. This is certainly not as I expected things to go. I hadn't expected that we would launch straight into an argument – apart from the last time I saw him, we have never fallen out over anything. "I said *needed*. If I had another option, I wouldn't *fucking be here!*"

He looks nonplussed. Of course, I appreciate that he has none of the information that has led me to that conclusion, but I am not about to let him off the hook.

"I've been over it, and guess what, buddy, you're the best of a fucking poor list."

"Been over what? What on earth are you even *talking about?* What's with that fucking suitcase?" He gesticulates with one arm toward the doorway, keeping his voice at the level of a forced whisper. To my credit, so am I.

"That *fucking* suitcase is all that I could bring with me. That *fucking* suitcase represents the rest of my fucking life. That *fucking* suitcase has got everything that I own in it. That *fucking* suitcase is all I have, and I am *asking* for your *fucking* help!"

Ok, so I may have over exaggerated the 'all of worldly possessions' angle, but I can see from his expression that he is beginning to show some concern. I spread my hands in front of me and lower them to the table, in a gesture of supplication.

"Look, I didn't want it to be like this. I need your help, Simon, and believe me, I wish I didn't, but you're the only person that I can turn to. I'm sick – really sick – and I am about to get a lot sicker."

To his credit I have his full attention for the next twenty minutes, not taking his eyes from me as I lay it all out for him – except for when the girlfriend comes into the kitchen all shoulder pads and power suit and tells him she will see him later and gives him another kiss on the mouth, before turning to me and saying it was nice to meet me. There is a smudge of bright red lipstick on him that he unconsciously reaches up and wipes it away with a thumb. Both of our coffees go cold, the half slice of toast goes uneaten. He doesn't say a thing during that time, except to Alina, and just listens.

I tell him about the lumps, the tests, the diagnosis, the prognosis, that I am expected at the hospital in three days' time to discuss when my treatment can begin and what that treatment will be. I tell him about the survivability statistics for people that have tumours in their lung, breast and lymph. The one-year statistics aren't good, even at my relatively young age. I start telling him about the side effects, and about losing my hair, and that's when I break and I cry and he gets up from his stool, comes around the end of the table and holds me, and I cry, and I cry, and I cry onto him.

Alina

The woman's suitcase is still there at the bottom of the stairs when I get home from work, as is Simon, it turns out. I know from the rota on the fridge that he was due on a later shift today, so the presence of his car on the driveway is almost as much of a mystery to me as her luggage is.

Entering the lounge, I can tell that there is something ill at ease here – the coffee table is strewn with empty mugs, and the focus of the room seems to be the stranger I met this morning, whose luggage is still here. Sure enough, there is Simon, but Ella is there too, clutching a mug. As ill at ease as I feel, I do not want this stranger to know it, so I throw my workbag into a vacant chair and Simon immediately stands up to give me a kiss on the cheek.

"You remember Denise from this morning?" he asks, somewhat redundantly. Of course I remember the strange woman turning up on my doorstep. I think I would be ill advised to say this though, and just nod and smile politely, in her general direction.

"Would you like a drink, darling?" he says, "tea, coffee...?" and he starts moving toward the kitchen. I know him well enough that this is his indication to me to follow.

"Ooo I need a coffee" I say.

"OK, so this is going to take some explaining" is his opening gambit once we're there. Whilst he makes a big fuss and far more noise than necessary making me a coffee, I get who Denise is and the bare bones of why she is here.

"So she wants to move in, is that it?" I hiss. Simon looks pained. "Well, actually... sort of yeah. But only until she can find something of her own. Look, we can't really talk about it right now, but I promise we will talk about it tonight, OK? Just for now can you treat this like a... like an unexpected house guest."

I am not happy about this, but I do know Simon well enough to know that whatever is going on here I will get the full story and that there are likely some good reasons for it, whatever 'it' is.

There is more than a little discomfort when I return with him to the lounge, so after a few minutes I take my coffee up to my room, with the not unreasonable, and entirely genuine, excuse that I need to get out of my shoes and into something comfortable. To his credit, Simon joins me no more than a few minutes later. When he enters the room, I have only got as far as sitting on the bed massaging the balls of my feet, which, again to his credit, he takes over for me as he sits next to me and draws my foot into his lap.

I am tired, and more than a little irritable, but I'll be honest, a foot rub was not the worst idea he could have come up with to make me feel in a slightly better mood. I appreciate we don't have long up here with our 'unexpected house guest' downstairs, but in our brief time he tells me that she is unwell, possibly severely so, and that according to her, she had no one else to reach out to except to an old friend. I know the answer before I have to push him on it, and he tells me that this is the same on-again off-again woman he once told me about but assures me at least three times before we return downstairs that that is something long since passed, swapping feet as he lays out what he knows about her unexpected appearance. Not that he needed to give me that assurance – we have lived together or worked together long enough that I would know if he were lying, and for all that this man is, he is not a liar – but it is not unwelcome.

I take off my suit and put on a pair of joggers and big t-shirt – one of Simon's that I took a shine to – to venture downstairs again, and I stand on tiptoe to give him a kiss and stroke his face before we head back down.

To both my surprise and, if I am totally honest with myself, no small amount of disappointment, the evening is not nearly as uncomfortable as I thought it might have been, and we all talk as though we are newly found friends. Mama keeps her distance, as does Christiana, neither of which is particularly unusual, and Denise seems at least outwardly pleased to meet Jack when Mama calls on me to bring him down. We don't talk about why she's here, and she doesn't seem overly willing to share with me, which, I suppose, is fine – to her I am someone she has only just met, albeit she is sitting in my home. Simon gets us all a Chinese takeaway which she eats very little of, and he opens a couple of bottles of red which she consumes a significant amount of, apparently with no noticeable ill effects. Ella makes her up a bed on the couch and after the obligatory 'the toilet is there, the kitchen is there, help yourself to anything you want' conversation, while she beds herself down, I lead Simon to his bed.

In the dark, me laying on his shoulder with his arm around me, in whispered conversations, he tells me what he knows – I ask him questions and he answers me to the best of his knowledge, which, after a while, I appreciate is not much right now. In my head I don't know what to make of our house guest, what her motivations are for coming here, what she expects from him or from any of us, and it is a little frustrating not to be able to get the answers.

I do fall asleep, though, in Simon's arms, and sleep right the way through until morning and the alarm. It is only with a little guilt that I realise that the baby monitor has been off all night.

Dee

I have deliberately left my phone on silent and in my coat pocket since leaving yesterday, and I am not surprised to see 40-something missed calls and about twice as many text messages on it when I do take it out – the messages are much the same, the pleas for me to return home, call back, let me know where you are. I don't, of course, and delete most of them without even reading them. I do feel some guilt at this, but I remind myself that I have thought this through, time and again.

I am left in the house with Ella that next day, she just happening to be on a day off and Simon and Alina leaving together for work, and I am surprised to learn that she is also with Simon – she describes herself as the 'new' girlfriend, and Alina the 'old' one. I attempt to pry a little but all I can get out of Ella is that they're all very happy, apparently. She asks me sensible questions about the diagnosis and what is likely to happen next, some of which I can answer and some I can't, but it does all seem to come from a place of genuine interest, as well as some degree of warmth or care that at first, I feel is misplaced, then weird, then genuine. It is then of no surprise when Ella volunteers over lunch – that she has made for us both – to accompany me to the next outpatient appointment, which is, according to the letter I had the sense to grab as I left, a treatment planning meeting. For once it is nice to have a conversation about one of my appointments without feeling like I am the one that needs to talk down the other, and the relief is such that I accept the offer. I even find myself sharing my 'no bra for appointments' strategy, and she jokes that she's never going to have that problem, making a comedic sad face whilst pushing up her own breasts through her vest. I laugh at this, as does she, and I couldn't have imagined that I would be laughing right now.

I get to meet more of the household that day too – an older woman who comes off as rather rude and dismissive of me, until Ella explains that that is Mama and she doesn't speak much English. There is another fit of giggles between us when I mistake this to mean that she is Ella's mother, and then Simon's mother, before reaching the, as it later is apparent, correct conclusion. I meet Christiana in passing, she pokes her head into the kitchen and says "Hi" to Ella when she comes home from school and nods and smiles nervously at me before she disappears off upstairs to, presumably, her room.

When Alina and Simon return home that night it is clear from their demeanour that some decisions have been made, and some discussions have been had – after dinner (Indian takeaway tonight, no wine) we assemble for a kind of summit meeting in the lounge and it seems that Simon has been voted in as spokesperson for the group, which I immediately presume has been by a majority of one vote from Alina and none to him. Not that it is any concern of mine anymore, but she seems to have more than a little control over him and this household than Ella's assertion, that she is his partner, would at first have indicated.

I mentally prepare myself for being back in my car by tomorrow at the latest.

Ella

I remember meeting like this before, and just like then, I think about Anna and how protective she can be, and I become determined to see to it that this does not become me, Simon, and Alina on one side of a wall, and Denise on the other. There was a time when Alina was the outsider and it was me that saw to it that she, and I, and Simon, were treated fairly. It is thanks to me that we have this life together because I was not willing to let go, yes, but also because I knew that anything else would be wrong.

I did not expect, when I met her just yesterday, that I would be able to see what has brought Denise here, back into Simon's and by default into our lives – but after a day of talking of everything and nothing, of listening to her story and the steps that have taken her here, I can see exactly why she had to come here, and why she should reasonably expect the respite she's seeking. I have been there; I have been where she is – knowing that you must leave and then the clarity that comes with that knowledge that you have to make that happen. I have been there; needing something that no one around me can provide.

When Simon asks us to come and sit at the dining table after dinner, I feel ready to stand up for this woman, to make my case for her, like I had to for Simon, and for me, and although she will probably never see it, for Alina too. If I hadn't made my stand for me, I would have lost Simon, and she would have done too, in time. I truly believe he would not have forgiven her for making him break his promise to me, no matter how good a father, co-parent, partner, or husband he might have made.

We are barely seated before I stand up and start speaking.

"I'm going with Denise to her next appointment, and I think she should stay here" I say, adding helpfully after a pause, as if clarity were needed "with us".

I realise at this point that I haven't got the first clue whether this was something that Denise had even considered, and looking around the table I can see she is surprised by my outburst. She also does not look like she is the only one.

"Ok, umm..." begins Simon, before I plough on with "I've thought it all through" I haven't, but I press on further, "and there is room enough to put another bed in my room if I squash up a bit, she can stay there."

"Ok, umm..." Simon begins again, after a pause, but I am getting into my stride a bit now.

"All of us needed one of us sometime – you needed him, even though you won't admit it, I needed him, he needed me... er... us, and he needed Jack, so, err... well, we all need people sometimes is what I think we should all... think about." I finish weakly and sit down and I can feel my face beginning to flush.

Simon clears his throat, and I think for a moment that he is going to stand up as well, but he doesn't – he shuffles a little uncomfortably in his seat until Alina rests her hand on his and he sits back still and steady.

"You're right" she says, simply.

There is a long pause while the four of us look back and forth at each other.

"So, Dee..." Simon begins.

"Denise" she says. "I never really liked Dee".

"So, Denise" he begins again, "I was going to tell you that you are more than welcome to stay for as long as you need, although we would need to work out the sleeping arrangements; however, it seems that Ella has worked all of that out for us." He pauses long enough to smile at me before he carries on. "It'll have to be the sofa until we can get a bed and move some furniture around, but you're welcome to stay. If you want to."

Alina

It has been some weeks since this stranger turned up at my door with nothing but a suitcase and a story, but for all my misgivings at the time, and now, I can at least acknowledge that the story is true. I would be lying if I said that this has been easy for me to accept, made no easier by watching – and in some cases listening to – the progression of her disease and the effects of her treatments.

Mama hates her being here – which she tells me often and loudly and doesn't care much who she says it in front of. I thank God that she has stubbornly refused to speak more than a few words of English in the house, although I know she understands a lot more than she ever says. Christiana, as the only other person who can understand what is being said, laps it up, and has developed a sneering, almost sniggering face around her that is really very unattractive.

"She'll be dead soon enough, though", says Mama after her the end of her latest tirade. Christiana snorts.

Unfortunately, though, I can't help but agree with a lot of what she says – I am not happy about her being here in my home. I have a constant internal battle between my own compassion for a woman who is, very likely, going to be dying in front of my eyes very soon, and my dislike for this person who has forced her way into being here. Sat there around the dining table – the dining table Simon and I chose together, I might add – I could feel nothing but contempt for this woman. How dare she come here?

I could see, though, before that conversation at the table even started, that I was not going to win a battle on this – Simon is a nicer person than I am, and Ella is even nicer than that; between them, I would have had no chance. Better to lean into the idea of her being here, I had thought – there'll be other battles to have another time, best to play the gracious host.

I really don't like it, though.

I have had to reflect, though, that the fact of the matter is that for all my protestations, all my misgivings about living with Simon and Ella, Ella was right. Even though I was the outsider when she suggested us living together, it is her that has stepped back since and I have felt that Simon, Jack and me have had the time, the space, the opportunity to become a family. I am, when I look back on it properly, grateful to her for this gift. I sometimes watch Simon with Jack – he has a smile for Jack that I have never seen on him before he met his son – our son.

Even Ella has become part of our not-so-little family, treating Jack as I imagine she would treat her own – she even took night duties in the early weeks just like Simon and me, and she has taken it all in her stride. Without her I very much doubt that I would have been able to get back to work so soon – with her, I feel secure enough to be at work and know that Mama and Ella are taking good care of our child.

But this Denise – who is she to us? She has not been through what we have been through together! She has no place here! She has had none of the commitments Simon, Ella and I have made to and for each other. But as I said, I knew as soon as I looked at them both where it was going to go. I did have my doubts, but I can see that for all his compassion, Simon has no feelings for her beyond sympathy for someone he knows being in trouble.

What I don't think I will ever understand, though, is why Ella fought so hard for her – fights so hard for her. She has thrown herself into caring for her, taking her to the endless appointments and therapy sessions, staying up late at night when Denise's symptoms are bad, doing her laundry, her shopping, her shoulder to cry on and her chauffeur, confidante, care worker and compatriot.

In my darkest moments, although I feared that she would be a threat to me and Simon, the threat has been to our unit which until now, I had barely noticed had formed. In my darkest moments, I feel like her cancer has become a cancer in my family that needs to be excised. For all the good that she is doing, I can see that supporting Dee has put a strain on the relationship between Ella and Simon – I know that for the last few weeks Ella has been distant to Simon. Of course I know how often they have shared his bed – I always do – and that has been significantly reduced these last months, a situation I have not exploited, as such, but certainly taken the opportunity to share in the comfort of his bed, his arms and his body next to mine more frequently than perhaps I had accustomed to, so for all my internal protestation I have to accept that there has been the benefit to me of his closeness, and it is in those moment that I remember that once, I chose to break his heart rather than accept my love for him, and then I have to remember what a foolish, foolish woman I was for doing that.

Denise

It has been an exhausting day. This is the roughest round of chemo I have had, and I know in myself that I am at a real low point. As I often do when I am feeling low these days, I self-consciously touch my scars – I slide my hand into my nightshirt and touch the scar where my breast used to be, and then reach round to the scar in my armpit. They're the only two – the tumour on the lung has proven resistant to whatever poisons and radiation modern medicine has thrown at it and has remained intractably large and present. The effort both hurts and tires me. I have tried to keep up with the therapies as much as possible, even when I have been advised that I might be better taking a break. I want this thing out of me, as soon as possible, and I am not afraid of a little hard work, or a little nausea – although in truth, it hasn't been just a little nausea.

I don't know what I really expected, turning up at Simon's house that day, but I know I did the right thing for me. These last few weeks have been rougher than my worst expectations. Every piece of new news was always the worst of any options. Every treatment has had more or worse side effects than even the doctors anticipated. The tumours have been more aggressive, more invasive than even the most pessimistic predictions.

Simon has been of practically no help at all – if I needed someone to detachedly quote statistics at me, or debate the benefits and drawbacks of a certain treatment with me, he would have been a godsend, but what the last few weeks have taught me is that I was looking for unconditional support, and that anything I ever had with him was always transactional.

But that was true of Ben, too. Even Becca. The relationship we had was, for all of them, what I could give as part of the deal. What I was prepared to give, I suppose. It doesn't matter now, anyway – the person that I was then is long since gone, leaving behind nothing but a disease-ridden shell that no one could now want anything from.

And that is why going to Simon has turned out to have been the right thing for me, because of Ella. From the day of the dining table summit meeting to this, she has wanted nothing from me. There is no give and take, I have been nothing but take and she has asked for, expected, wanted nothing in return. Having me for a roommate cannot have been a joy for her, especially not when she has helped clean me up in the middle of the night after I have vomited all over myself or bled from a surgical wound all over the sheets, or when I cried in self-pity and self-loathing for hours on end.

She has been there at every outpatient appointment, every admission, and every discharge. This young woman who doesn't know a thing about me except that I was in need, she has been the one that has provided the care that I hoped I'd find when I threw my life into a suitcase.

She visits me most days, either before or after her shift at the hospital, and cares from me better than the workers on the ward. I have long since given up telling her that other people will manage my personal care when I can't, to which she always replied that they won't do it to her standards and I have to admit, she is probably right about that.

"Commitment is all we have" she once said to me, when I made some sort of ill-advised but well-meaning joke about getting all this professional care for free.

"What do you mean?" I asked.

"Commitment is all we have" she repeated but could clearly see I didn't understand what she meant.

"We all choose the commitments we make – commitment to do a job well, to be a good person, to... to... go to church on Sunday's. We choose our commitments, the things that we value, the things that are right to us. Simon made a commitment to me" this is the first time that we have ever even touched on anything more about their relationship then I have seen for myself, "and I made a commitment to do the right thing. By him and because of him, by you. He isn't perfect, but he is mine and I will always help him to make the right commitments too. We all choose our commitments."

We lapsed into silence after that, as I remembered the commitments I made and ignored, and the commitments I should have made but didn't. To be fair, as I spend an awful lot of my time in bed these days, I have little to do except to reflect on things and think about what things I could have, should have done differently.

I am in a reflective mood when Ella arrives at lunch time with a Tupperware container and wielding a spoon. She helps me to sit up, although as weak as I am it is really more like I barely help her to sit me up, and we talk about nothings while she coaxes me into eating something.

I have been sleeping since Ella left – she did manage to get some soup that she had made into me, and most of it has stayed down. I have often marvelled at this woman who has no reason to lift a finger for me yet has been such a continual source of support.

I have not been able to keep much track of the time, but I imagine it must be early evening – there is no clock or watch within my private bubble behind the curtains, but I can see the sun is pretty low, as we are heading into autumn, and I can see it shining on the hospital curtains around my bed. There's more movement than usual outside the curtains and the bay and I assume that it must be the start of visiting hours. I expect to see Simon later – he told me at the weekend that he would be on duty today, and it is not unusual for him to come and visit me on my admissions before he goes home.

I lift my head and try to shuffle into a more comfortable position, but the effort is too much, and I flop back onto the pillow. I hold my hand up to the light coming through the curtains and I can swear that I can see the light passing right through it now, my flesh seeming almost translucent. What on earth happened to that young woman that I once was? I smile to myself as I recall Becca and what she used to say about me, and I agree that I did have a cracking bod. More of a creaking bod these days... I'll have to remember that line for the next time I speak to her.

I drift in and out for a bit, but I am stirred into wakefulness by a voice I recognise but haven't heard in months, calling name softly. I begin to dream – one of those dreams where I never quite know if I am dreaming or am awake. It seems real, but the edges are fuzzy, like they're obscured by clouds no matter which way I look. Like in a dream I don't feel my body – but this is a blessed relief. I dream that I open my eyes, and I look up to see Ben – my Ben. I weakly try to lift up my arms to him, but he seems out of reach and I can sense that he hesitates, and then I remember that he hasn't seen me for months and instead I self-consciously pat my head where my hair used to be and then drop my twig-like arms down to my sides. I am about to turn myself away when he seems to glide up to my bedside and gathers me up in his arms. From the corner of my eye and through the gap in the curtains, until unbidden tears blur the view, I see the nurse outside nod to herself and move off. The best I can do is lift my hands up to his shoulders and hold him, but there is little strength there – but I want to hug him and hold him tighter than ever.

"I'm sorry, I'm sorry" I croak repeatedly, my throat and mouth feeling terribly dry. As tearful reunions go, I am underwhelmed by my ability to do much more than this. He lowers me gently back to the bed but stays standing.

"Sit" I say, indicating a high-backed chair that has appeared at the bedside. He does and shuffles it closer so that he can hold my hand. I squeeze it – although so little am I aware of my body and such is my weakness that I am not sure whether he would have felt it, even if this were real.

The effort of all this movement and excitement seems to cause me to lose focus and suddenly he is standing again, drifting further away from me. I wave my hand in the direction of a beaker of squash with a straw in it and then he is there again, drifting up to the bedside, taking up the beaker and bringing the straw to my lips. Between sips, I say "How?"

"Becca told me", he says, softly. "She came round and told me that I should come and see you and where you were." The words seem to come from a long distance away.

"I bet she didn't tell you the state I was in, did she?"

"She did, which is why she thought I should come. Denise," and he falters a little bit here, "why? Why leave? Why leave me? Where have you been?". His eyes are red-rimmed but dry. He has cried all the tears he has for me today – I wonder if there were many.

I try to stay with the dream, but I can feel it, me, slipping away – the clouding of my dream vision seems to be getting thicker, and it see the dream through a smaller and smaller circle.

I think that I pat the hand that is holding my right hand with my left, and then I tell him that he is here and that is all that counts. I tell him that in my moment of greatest need that he has come through for me as I should have known that he would. I tell him that I should never have walked out on him, that despite my own fears I should have known that he would be there for me, as he always has been. I tell him I should have been true to my commitment to him, all that time ago. I ask for his forgiveness for having treated him so badly for so many years, for running around behind his back, for disrespecting him, for being dishonest with him and for being distant to him. At least, I would tell him those things if I had the breath and the strength, so I have to hope that the pat communicates these things to him, and instead I just say that I am sorry again. And I am sorry, too.

I think that he asks me how I have been, and in my dream, the arm that no longer seems to belong to me reaches up to my bare scalp again. "Better" I say, and smile at him. I used to be able to read this man like a book, but today I can't tell what he is thinking.

He reaches up to the top of the cabinet he is sitting by and pulls down a box of tissues, pulling one out and dampening it from the water jug on the bedside table. He reaches over and wipes away something from the corner of my mouth – probably some of that small portion of soup that was determined not to stay down – then looks around for somewhere to discard it. Not seeing anywhere, he bundles the tissue up and puts it in his jacket pocket, then he leans over and kisses me gently, tenderly, lovingly, on the lips. I can't remember the last time I was kissed; never mind the last time I was kissed with such love.

"I'm sorry" I say again. "Ben, I am so tired. I am so broken. I have been so terrible to you." I try to lift my hand to his face, and instead, he lifts his to hold it there a moment. I can't feel him, my hand may as well be touching the clouds that reach ever in to obscure my vision.

He sits, but he is still holding on to my right hand. I try to read his face again, but there is nothing there to read. Perhaps it is because I am so tired, and for all that I wouldn't get through the day without the morphine I know I don't think as clearly with it.

"Ben?" I say.

"Yes, my love?"

"Will you sit with me while I dream? I am sorry but I am so tired, we can talk more when I am more awake."

"Of course, my love" he replies, and strokes my cheek with the back of his fingers.

I close my eyes and let the clouds take me. I can almost feel my hand in his. I can feel myself drifting off deeper. I can feel his forehead when he touches it against mine.

Simon

It's later than I had planned by the time I finish my shift – I'm held up by an all-hands-to-the-pump emergency about 15 minutes before I had planned to leave – a four-car accident with nine patients of varying age and trauma – so it is getting close to the end of visiting hours by the time I make my way upstairs to the ward. I take the lift instead of the stairs – although it is only one floor, I have been on my feet most of the day and I think I have deserved the minimal rest that this allows.

Sure enough, I have arrived only just in time. It isn't quite closing time yet, but some visitors are leaving as I walk in – I pass a couple corralling some children out of the door; one of the kids briefly escapes her handler and runs back to wave at someone from the doorway of the bay, before returning to her mother's side. I can see some other people making their arrangements to leave through the glass, picking up coats and bags, hugging, kissing, a final little wave. I wonder for how many people that that will be a final wave. I am briefly jostled by a man about my age, and I turn to say something, but he has run into me because his head is low and he is clearly distraught, so hasn't seen me. I watch his retreating back for a moment as he hurries off.

I carry on down to the end of the ward – I have learned that longer term patients are usually put at the far end, where it is quieter and there is less bustle – and it means you can also judge how sick you are based on how far along the ward your bed is. There are a handful of single occupancy rooms on the left and one four-person bay on the right. Dee is in the bay, so her illness hasn't quite graduated her to a single occupancy room, but far enough.

As I approach the bay, I can see that the curtains have been drawn around her bed except for a gap of about a foot at the corner closest to me. Of course, this is a terrible breach of hospital protocol where curtains have to be left open so that the patients – and, in fairness, visitors – can be seen from the corridor, but I know Dee enjoys the privacy and I think nothing of it. Usually, curtains around a bed mean one of two things, either that a staff member is with the patient, or the patient is beyond the help of any staff member every again.

I put my head and shoulders into the gap, and I can see that she is sleeping, so I enter quietly and leave the curtains drawn. I sit in the chair that is already next to the bed and feel it is uncomfortably warm, as though someone has just got out of it. Dee doesn't stir. Her hand is laid by her side, so I gently take it in mine so as not to disturb her.

Her hand feels cool. She makes no move. It's then I notice in the dim light that the skin on her hand has taken a waxy sheen, and that her mouth is slack. And that her chest isn't moving. I leap up so that the chair scrapes on the floor as it is pushed away from me and place my ear over her mouth – nothing. No sounds, no movement. I reach for the emergency pull and my fingers curl around the button and then I stop.

Where I have leapt up, I have allowed her hand to fall from the bed, and it dangles, lifelessly, from the side.

I let go of the emergency pull. I recover the chair, sit down and I take hold of her hand again, bringing it back onto the bed, and I quietly begin to tell her about my day as I stroke the back of her hand with my thumb.

I am glad that the curtains are drawn because the staff will have to come and find me if they want me to leave.

September 2014

Printed in Great Britain
by Amazon